We Are Their Voice

A Holocaust Remembrance Book for Young Readers

We Are Their Voice

Young People Respond to the Holocaust

Created and Edited by
Kathy Kacer

with Karen Krasny, Alan Gotlib,
Susan Gordin, and Shawntelle Nesbitt

Second Story Press

Library and Archives Canada Cataloguing in Publication

Kacer, Kathy, 1954-
We are their voice : young people respond to the Holocaust / by Kathy Kacer.

(The Holocaust remembrance series for young readers)
ISBN 978-1-926920-77-1

1. Holocaust, Jewish (1939-1945)—Influence—Juvenile literature.
I. Title. II. Series: Holocaust remembrance book for young readers.

D804.34.K338 2012   j940.53'18   C2012-904034-7

Edited by Sheba Meland
Cover illustration by Maria Basso-Jimenez, Gr.7,
Regina Mundi Catholic School, Hamilton, Ontario
Cover and text design by Melissa Kaita
Printed and bound in Canada

*The views or opinons expressed in this book and the context in which the
images are used, do not necessarily reflect the views or policy of, nor imply approval
or endorsement by, the United States Holocaust Memorial Museum.*

*Second Story Press gratefully acknowledges the support of the Ontario Arts Council
and the Canada Council for the Arts for our publishing program. We acknowledge
the financial support of the Government of Canada through the Canada Book Fund.*

Published by
SECOND STORY PRESS
20 Maud Street, Suite 401
Toronto, ON M5V 2M5
www.secondstorypress.ca

"…love is better than anger. Hope is better than fear. Optimism is better than despair. So let us be loving, hopeful, and optimistic. And we'll change the world."

Jack Layton, 2011
Former leader of the New Democratic Party, Canada

"When they are gone, we are their voice."

Ori Berman
Grade 8 student
Leo Baeck Day School (North Campus), Toronto

Contents

Introduction 1

Foreword 4

What is Happening to Us? 7

Can We Stay Together? 23

Where Will We Hide? 40

The Fear Is Overwhelming! 50

The Goodness of Some 61

Not Everyone Is Willing to Help 85

How Will We Ever Survive? 99

It Comes Down to Luck 117

We Have to Have Hope 127

Looking for Justice 151

Fighting Back 166

We Are Their Voice 174

Putting Words into Actions 195

Glossary 211

References 222

Members of the Panel 225

Participating Schools 229

Acknowledgments 231

To all the students who wrote stories and drew pictures
This book is yours.

Introduction

This is a collection of very moving, often even heart-wrenching writing and drawings created by young people like you. It is unlike any other book you will ever read. I have been writing books about the Holocaust for many years, trying to preserve this important history and find a way for others to learn from this horrific event. I am also the child of Holocaust survivors. My mother survived the war in hiding, and my father was a survivor of the concentration camps, so keeping this history alive is very personal for me. The survivors of the Holocaust are aging and, all too soon, their voices will be gone. I wondered – could a new generation pick up that baton and be the voice of this history and of those who lived through it?

A Spanish-American philosopher named George Santayana once said, "Those who cannot learn from history are doomed to repeat it."[1]

---

[1] Santayana, George. *The Life of Reason*, Volume I, New York: Prometheus Books, 1998.

Santayana was concerned that once history was written, we would stop inquiring into past events so that we might continue to learn from them. I would like to think that as a society we have learned a lot since the time of the Holocaust. I would like to believe that we have learned to be kinder to one another, to stop fighting and killing and discriminating against those who are different. But sadly, this is not the case. The world continues to be plagued with war, genocides, and ongoing racial discrimination. Now more than ever, we must find a way to understand the evil events of history that keep repeating. This is the only way that we will be able to work toward a more equitable and peaceful world.

In the spirit of that ongoing goal, I created a writing opportunity for young people like you, across Canada, parts of the United States, and Europe. This project asked students in grades 6, 7, and 8 to write about the Holocaust in a meaningful way – to try to understand the impact of this event, and to translate that into a story, a reflection, a response to a book or photo, a journal entry, a letter, or a tribute to a survivor. A wonderful committee of educators worked with me to develop the guidelines for young people to participate. Schools had to sign a letter of commitment for their students to take part. Each of those schools that signed on submitted their top five pieces of writing to me and my committee. I guaranteed that at least one out of five of those submissions would be published.

We Are Their Voice: Young People Respond to the Holocaust is the result of this effort. The book you are beginning contains the eighty-five pieces of writing that were chosen from more than two hundred submissions. In addition, there are a dozen drawings here that students also created.

As a committee, we were overwhelmed with the sensitivity, thoughtfulness, and insight that young people brought to this writing project. As you can imagine, selecting these eighty-five pieces was incredibly difficult. The final choices fill this collection with dramatic wisdom from your fellow students – and provide important lessons and reflections about this terrible time in history.

Despite the fact that it happened long before you were born, you *can* make a meaningful connection to the Holocaust. And perhaps, with that in mind, you will be able to create a more peaceful future. Read the stories. Listen to the hopes, fears, and dreams that have been expressed here. We have so much to learn from you, the young people of the world.

Kathy Kacer

Foreword

I met Kathy Kacer for the first time several years ago. As a Holocaust survivor and World War II veteran, I have been speaking in schools and libraries for years, telling my personal story.[2] I have collected thousands of poems, letters, drawings, and photographs that students have sent to me after hearing me speak. I contacted Kathy, wondering if there was anything that could be done with this collection of material. Little did I know that at about the same time, Kathy was thinking of creating a book of stories about the Holocaust written by young people. She asked me if I would write a foreword to this book when it was completed. I was happy to accept.

I was born in Rokitno, Poland (now Ukraine), and lived my childhood in a loving family. But when the Nazis took over in 1941,

---

[2] Alex has written about his life in his memoir, *Under the Yellow and Red Stars*, Azrielli Foundation, Toronto, 2009.

everything changed. Almost every Jewish person in my town was murdered, including my parents. My older brother Samuel and I managed to escape into the forest, and we survived there together in unbelievable and unbearable conditions. But we did survive. And I have spent my life since then talking about the Holocaust, and trying to keep the memory of this time alive.

In my vocabulary, *hate* is a word that does not exist. Now, if you had asked me about this at the time that I lost my family, I might have said something else. But that was a different time, and I was a different person. I have learned that it is useless to try to fight bigotry with more bigotry. Hate only leads to more hate. That's not to say that it isn't important to fight back against injustice. Of course it is. Even in your own schools, you must fight for those who are being attacked or put down for their differences. You can never be quiet about these things. But you must speak up in ways that provide positive solutions. Understanding the stories of those of us who survived the Holocaust will, I hope, enable you to speak up for others who are unjustly targeted, in the future.

I always tell students that I am not here to teach about the Holocaust. I say to them: you already have many teachers, and my hope is that they will give you information about this time in history, or that you will learn about the events that happened during that time on your own. So I am not a teacher. I am here to tell you my personal story. And my hope is that it will be meaningful to you – it will touch you in a way that facts cannot. And if you are moved by my recollections and those of other survivors, then my hope is that you will want to know more, and do more in your own life to fight against the prejudices that exist in the world. In many ways, my work is like the message of this book.

We Are Their Voice is a moving collection of stories written by young people who have connected with the history of the Holocaust in a powerful way. And if you think about it, we can all be the voice of this history – you and me both. I will continue to tell my personal story for as long as my brain is working and I am able to speak. I do this not for myself, but for those who are gone, and for you, the next generation. Now I hope you will want to keep the meaning of the Holocaust alive in your own way, and help make a better and more just world for all.

Alex Levin, Toronto
June, 2012

Chapter 1

What is Happening to Us?

Try to imagine what life was like for Jewish families in Europe before the start of the Second World War. I know that was a long time ago, and it's hard to picture life in the 1920s or '30s. The truth is, aside from having the technology that most of us enjoy today, the life of a Jewish family in Europe was probably not all that different from yours. The men and women worked in professions such as medicine, teaching, law, construction, politics, or business. Jewish children went to school and spent free time in the playgrounds and parks. Siblings and friends did things together and probably even disagreed at times. Jewish families ate meals around the table, went on vacations, and celebrated holidays and birthdays. Jewish people then had all of the rights that we have today, rights that many of us take for granted. Now imagine that those freedoms that allow us to do the things we do every single day begin to disappear, one by one.

One of the most important things to understand is that the Holocaust did not begin with the building of the six major death camps across Poland and Germany from 1939-1945. It did not start when Hitler sat down with his commanders in 1942 to develop his Final Solution – the annihilation of the Jews of Europe. The Holocaust really began much earlier, when Hitler came to power in 1933 and began to implement laws and rules that restricted the freedom of Jewish people and others. These laws seemed quite mild at first: Jews can't go to the same parks as others, or play in the playgrounds, or attend movie theaters. Many Jewish people believed that if they followed these rules, things would not get worse and the restrictions would eventually be lifted. The Nazis were very good at keeping all the information about the Final Solution secret. While Hitler publicly said that he wanted Europe, and indeed the whole world, to be free of Jews, he never talked openly about the gas chambers, and the brutality that Jews would face in the concentration camps. When Jews were being deported to these fearsome places, they were fooled into believing that they were going to be sent to new towns, where they would find work and be reunited with loved ones who had been deported ahead of them.

Very few people could see that the earlier rules were just the beginning of a longer and more dangerous set of restrictions, each one intended to control the activity of Jews to such an extent that by the time the death camps were in place and people realized that their very lives were at risk, it was too late to escape.

The stories that you will read in this chapter reflect the creeping awareness that many Jewish people had about the dangers around them.

They couldn't understand what was happening to them, nor why. Most refused to believe that their countries would ever desert them in the face of rising anti-Semitism. They could see that things were different, but firmly believed that they could ride out the problems and eventually everything would return to normal. They loved their homes, their families, their neighborhoods, their schools and synagogues. They never imagined that they would lose everything as the war approached. Read on to see what your fellow students felt about these fearful times.

Allie Fenwick, Gr.8
Robbins Hebrew Academy, Toronto, Ontario

The Diary of Eve Rosenheim

September 3, 1942

Mama says that the Nazis have begun to search the small town in which we are *existing* – to call it *living* would be a ridiculous stretch. We must run! As I write these words, I sit in the corner of a small, damp basement that can only be accessed via a locked trapdoor. A table and stools furnish the room, along with one candlestick, our only source of light. The only reason that Mama, my brother, Noah, and I stick our heads out of the trapdoor in the low ceiling is so that Mr. Avianson, the nice Catholic man who hides us and helps us, can give us our meals. We sleep wherever and whenever we can. Mama and Noah look as if they are about to die of starvation any moment now, and I know I must look the same. But we are strong. Every day when I wake up with aches and pains and my stomach grumbling, I tell myself that if a human being can live like this, surely he can withstand even more.

Wait. Is it September? I used to start school in this month! Yes, now I remember a dream from last night. How could I have forgotten this! In my dream, I am walking to class with some girls, but they have no faces. In fact, everyone else I see in my dream is faceless too. We pass the trophy case, and I can see my own reflection. My face has been replaced with a Star of David, a nice one with gold edges and an opal center. Suddenly, men with spider-like insignias for heads run into the hallways. They are armed. I recognize the spider insignia. It is the swastika. Two of the men grab my arms and drag me out the doors. I try to scream for help, but no words come out of my mouth. I kick wildly, but my limbs go straight through the men's bodies as if they are made of air. They throw me into the back of a truck and shut the doors. Inside the dark and damp vehicle, I notice that the air is thick and smelly, as if there is gas – and I suddenly realize there is! I collapse, and the world spins and fades before my eyes. I am struggling to recall the prayers from synagogue when a man wearing dirty, bloody army clothes appears before me. He says in a soothing voice, "Just a little longer, child. The Allies will stop this prejudice or die trying." As he says this last sentence, I feel as though my lungs have been shocked back to life.

In my dream, I slowly stand up. I realize that the man is gone and I am back at school playing hopscotch with my friends – my real friends, not those faceless fakes. And then, I am at my dinner table at home. I am with my family, and I am eating the most delicious thick, hearty stew I have ever tasted. Even Papa is there.

That's my dream. But even though it is all in my head, I believe that the man in army clothes is right. Just a little longer. Our freedom shall come. Until then, I wait. I don't care how long – a week, a month or a year.

Chelsea Chettleburgh, Gr.6
O.M. MacKillop Public School, Richmond Hill, Ontario

Before the War

August 1, 1938

Hello my name is Hana. This is my very first diary entry, so I'll just introduce myself. I'm eight years old and live in Berlin with my parents and my eleven-year-old brother, Karl. I love to go to school every day and play in the park.

September 15, 1938

Diary, we need help! Life is terrible now with all the laws the Nazis have placed upon us. I'm heartbroken! Papa's business is no more. I don't know why. But I overheard my parents saying that the Nazis made a law that Germans can't buy from Jewish businesses. I don't know everything because my parents think I'm a little too young to understand. I did hear them say that the Nazi soldiers have forbidden us to go wherever we want and stripped us of our citizenship. Everything we once had has been slowly taken away. Does this mean I'm not a person? How will I get a job when I'm grown up? What will this do to my parents? What will happen when I'm an adult and want to have a family? I worry about my cousins and my aunt and uncle. It's like the Nazis are not letting us into the game everyone is playing – but this is no game. It's my life! Let me pray to God to help me get through this.

September 29, 1938

A lot has changed! I don't know exactly where I am, but our family ran away and is hiding. We have to stay in a small building with other Jewish people. I don't like staying in here because I love to play in the park with my friends. Still, this is safer than the streets of Berlin. I wonder what it is like for the other Jews still living there. I hope they're okay. I overheard that if we get caught something bad will happen to us and I wonder what the Nazis will do. I hope that no one hurts us; we're all people after all. But the Nazis are mean. Even though we're safe in this place for now, my older brother, Karl, doesn't talk very much. He used to have a fun personality. He would take me to the park after school. Now he is sad and quiet. I wonder if my parents think he is old enough and told him what the Nazis might do to us. Nothing is the same as it used to be.

Colin Rak, Gr.7
St. Nicholas Catholic School, Waterloo, Ontario

Honoring the Survivors

Dear Survivors,

I cannot imagine all the pain you went through during the Holocaust. In my simple, everyday life if I hear of just one death on the news I can barely choke back my tears. It makes me hurt inside, just knowing of all these terrifying events. What did it feel like for you when you realized that so many Jewish people were being killed? At first you were banned from participating in everyday activities. I can't think of how badly you felt being barred from stores and shunned in your community. It horrifies me to hear that all of these terrible things happened to you, merely because of your religious beliefs and heritage.

How hopeless you must have felt being taken from your home, your family, and being shipped to concentration camps. How terrible to be forced to do hard labor against your will and to watch others die. I have no idea how I could handle even a few days in these appalling living conditions. Being starved and hurt would make me feel worthless. The Jewish people were born into this world and should be welcomed here just as much as any other living beings. It also sickens me to think that the Nazis murdered young children. Some who were killed were so young they had no idea what was happening to them. How could the Nazis do such things to innocent beings?

Even though today we are educated about the Holocaust, I don't think that people understand how terrifying these times were for so many. I know that in some places around the world they have a day to remember the lives that were lost. We are all still scared that these events could be repeated. That is why there is an international day to honor Holocaust survivors, and to remember why this event is such an important part of our world's history.

I hope that events like the Holocaust will never happen again, and I hope that the ones that were hurt the most are able to find peace and live a fulfilled life.

Katie Sutter, Gr.7
St. Nicholas Catholic School, Waterloo, Ontario

The Pink Triangle

I stepped out onto our front porch, dazed, and tried to adjust my eyes to the bright morning sunlight. It was a lazy Sunday morning. My sister and I had stayed up late the previous night celebrating, and as a special treat, we had been allowed to sleep in.

"Ivan! Good morning!" I heard a powerful yell coming from down the road. It was Martin, the son of a couple who lived on the farm next to us. My heart flipped a bit. He was my friend, of course, but there was another strange feeling I had. I couldn't identify it, or even acknowledge it. We were just two boys who were friends and were growing up in the Polish countryside together.

Martin came over and slapped my back. I stumbled a bit. He was a strong, handsome young man, with tousled sandy hair, and bright gray eyes. I, on the other hand, was a lanky kid, with curly brown hair, mossy green eyes, and freckles sprinkled over my face. If you stood us together, you'd think Martin was twenty years old, instead of sixteen, and I, fourteen instead of sixteen.

It was 1940, and news of the war was spreading, but since we were both Christians, we felt we had less to fear. On that particular day, Martin and I stood together for a while, sharing gossip and chit-chat. We noticed some people in town wearing a yellow Star of David. When I asked Martin about it, he said they were Jews. Then we saw someone wearing a badge that was different. It was pink and in the shape of a triangle. When I asked Martin why this badge was different, he wouldn't answer and changed the subject.

Later that evening, my family and I sat in the sitting room. My

parents were discussing the news that all Jewish people, gypsies, homosexuals, and others had to go to a particular station and pick up a badge
to identify themselves. I remembered that conversation with Martin and
it struck me – that feeling I had every time I saw or thought about him
finally emerged from the shadows of my mind. I realized that this was
something that I would no longer be able to hide.

I stood again on our front porch the next day. I took a deep breath,
and bravely opened the door. My mother was there to greet me. Her face
sank and her mouth hung open as she reached toward me and touched
the pink triangle sewn onto my jacket.[3]

Annika Ah-Chow, Gr.8
Gordon B. Attersley Public School, Oshawa, Ontario

Honor Their Memory

Adolf Hitler was always interested in politics, and his irrational hatred
of the Jews began early in his life. By the time Hitler became Chancellor
at the age of 44, his deadly intentions were unmistakable. He began his
evil plans slowly. Jews were allowed to shop only at certain stores, were
given specific benches to sit on, and their passports were marked with
an oversized "J". Segregation from German society became a reality for
the Jews. Eventually this escalated to more horrific deeds, ending with
the "Final Solution."

The Nazi soldiers forced Jewish people out of their homes. Men,

---

[3] Even though it is important to talk about the Pink Triangle, few people would have
voluntarily identified themselves as gay at that time. People who were homosexual were
often turned in by others.

women, and children were herded into cramped cattle trains and transferred to concentration camps. Many died on the trains due to lack of sanitation, food, and air. If they survived, they were used as slaves in the camps and tortured. Eventually, the survivors were brought to extermination camps such as Belzec, Treblinka, and Auschwitz-Birkenau.

The Holocaust finally ended in 1945 as the Allied forces overtook the Nazis. Of the nine million Jews who lived in Europe before the Second World War, only three million were still alive. At first, the survivors thought they were lucky to be alive, but then they had to cope with the reality of all the people they had loved and lost. Hitler's ways had spread throughout Europe. He was responsible for the deaths of over six million Jewish people and millions of others. What gave him the right to decide which race, religion, or nationality was superior to another? When Hitler found out he had been conquered, he took the coward's way out and committed suicide.

"Those who cannot learn from history are doomed to repeat it." This statement is very true. The Holocaust started when Jews were targeted by others. In recent years, we have heard about other countries targeting their own people due to racial, ethnic, and religious differences. Cambodia, Somalia, Armenia, and Rwanda are just a few of the many examples. People in these countries have been murdered, tortured, and raped. Imagine waking up every morning, feeling afraid, not knowing if you or your loved ones will ever live to see another day, or ever feel the warmth of the sun again. Innocent lives continue to be lost. People are being forced into hiding trying to keep themselves alive, much like what Anne Frank did in her attempt to survive. The United Nations states,

"All people are born free and equal in dignity and rights." Yet, people today are still forced to fight for freedom, safety, and the right to openly practice their religion.

One religious group is targeted because someone thinks his or her religion is superior, yet no one is better than anyone else. The day we truly start to believe that, will be the day we see a change in our world.

We must never forget the lives that were lost during the Holocaust and other genocides throughout history. Let us honor their memory by taking a stand against racism and injustice. As Martin Luther King Jr. said, "We must learn to live together as brothers, or perish together as fools."[i]

Melissa Mercuri-Amato, Gr.8
Pope John Paul II Elementary School, Bolton, Ontario

Thinking about Discrimination

My 5th grade class saw a video called *A Class Divided,*[ii] which is about a teacher named Jane Elliott who worked in a school in Iowa. This teacher had been thinking about how some people tease or mistreat others just because of the way they look, act, or talk. She decided to teach her students about discrimination using an exercise.

The teacher separated the class into those who had blue eyes and those with brown eyes. She said that the brown-eyed people were better than the blue-eyed people for many reasons. Though none of this was true, the class took it seriously and there were some pretty bad experiences between kids who had once been best friends! Blue eyes were seen as "weird" or "bad," and blue-eyed students even had to wear a green collar to make them feel more embarrassed. The students turned on one another within a few minutes of the discrimination exercise. When it was recess, the brown-eyed kids received ten extra minutes outside, while those with blue eyes had to stay in their seats. They felt terrible about themselves and didn't even do very well in their schoolwork.

The next day the teacher told the students that everything she had said the day before was wrong. Actually it was the blue-eyed people who were better than the brown-eyed people. Everyone switched places. Now brown-eyed people were the ones who felt bad about themselves. At recess, two boys had a fight because of their eye color. When they came inside, the teacher asked what had happened. The brown-eyed boy yelled that the blue-eyed boy had called him names. When it was time for reading groups, Ms. Elliott did the same as the day before and separated the groups by eye color. This time, the brown-eyed students did poorly in their work and those with the blue eyes did very well.

After watching this video, I could definitely understand how being told you are bad or don't belong could make you feel sad and less motivated. On the other hand, being told you're the best person in the whole world could make you feel as if you can achieve whatever you want.

This film made me think about the Holocaust. Both situations have similar patterns. During the war, Jews had to wear a yellow star on their clothing so that others were aware they were Jewish. At the school in Iowa, the "bad-eyed" students had to wear green collars, and that made them feel even more uncomfortable. These two situations connect in a way that made me feel sad about any kind of discrimination.

Everyone in the whole world should watch *A Class Divided*, and I wish everyone in the world could go through a similar exercise. It might be a positive start to make the terrible, unfair, hurtful, discrimination pattern stop.

Kathryn Wartski, Gr.5
Durant Rd. Elementary School, Raleigh, North Carolina

Danica's Story
April 10, 1942
Dear Diary,

In a few days, it'll be my birthday. I'm turning twelve. The war is still raging outside this dark, cold cellar. We're a family of four living beneath the streets of Warsaw, Poland. It isn't the perfect family home, especially not for a mother, a sick father, a little sister, Natia, and me, someone who is sick and tired of all these "Jews are evil" lies.

I used to love my life. Being Jewish made me proud and I had lots of friends. Now it's exceedingly lonely. As soon as the Nazis came, I was forbidden from being seen with my best friend, Felcia. She was the nicest person I had ever met. When I was taken away from her, I was furious. This was when my hatred started to build up against the Nazis who were now taking away my life. Every night I have written in you, Diary, and considered revenge. But I cannot think of any plans. The only thing I know is that if they take me away from you...No. Never will they pry me from my family, my thoughts, and my diary.

A few people so far have come stumbling back from where they were taken, and screamed for us to help others who are being killed. I have not seen this, but Tesia told us what she heard. It's Tesia's home that we are hiding in. Outside her bedroom window she hears the occasional cries of escapees before they are killed. The crack of a gunshot, the snap of a broken neck. Not one beaten-up prisoner escapes the horrid torture. Tesia tries to promise me I will live, but I doubt it. She has also told me about how they've been taking more and more Jews, more and more frequently. I sometimes have nightmares about the walls falling in and the Nazis standing here in front of us, dangling the bodies of those closest to me over their shoulders – Felcia, Natia, Tesia, my mother, my father, and my friends' parents as well. I keep having that dream. And every time, there's another body. I had the dream again last night. The whole town was under their will. They'll find us soon, I can feel it. Tesia has said something about a Nazi patrol group coming to all of the homes on this street to do a search. I'm scared. I might not live to be 12! And Natia, she's so young! Oh, I hope she lives. But, what if it's just to face loneliness like she's never imagined? That would not go well with her. Natia's so fragile.

Tesia looks worried. Of course she should be, because *she* is the one giving us a home, if you could call this home. It's shelter at least, from the Nazis, the traitors, the weather. I feel as if I should be stronger. I am very protective, but with the patrol coming I feel small, weak, as if I should be working harder to guard my family. My mother has always been shy, not a good trait for fighting. And I'm starting to think that Papa is about to give up his battle with illness, so as not to be forced into something that would surely kill him. He is thin. I don't think he's been eating. The

Nazis won't tolerate that. They'll finish him off as soon as they find us. That is why he would rather die from his sickness than bleed to death from a gunshot wound. The Nazis are that cruel. I am pretty sure that Papa is in pain. If, or rather, *when* they find us, I will try to protect my family. If I do not succeed, and they drag us out, I promise I will only go kicking, screaming, biting, and fighting for my life.

Shira Rubinoff, Gr.6
Downtown Jewish Community School, Toronto, Ontario

Chapter 2

Can We Stay Together?

Can you imagine what it would be like to be separated from your parents, your siblings, your friends or other family members? Can you imagine what it would be like if your parents were forced to send you away? Even if they told you that this was for your own good, or to save your life, would you really accept that and be willing to go? And would you actually have a choice?

As the war was advancing across Europe, those Jewish families who had not managed to get out of their home countries were now trying to find safe places to hide from the growing dangers. But it was nearly impossible to find places where entire families could hide together. So parents were often faced with the agonizing decision to send their children away. In many cases, these young Jewish children were sent to stay with strangers. Their parents did not know who these people were, or if they would treat their children kindly and lovingly. And at the time, these young Jewish children never knew when, or if, they would ever see their family members again.

Some children actually had to hide their identity – their real name, place of birth, religion – in order to live safely with their new "families." If you've ever been in a school play, or dressed up for a Hallowe'en party, then you know what it's like to pretend to be someone else. Now imagine doing that but also knowing that your life will depend on your ability to stay in character. You will have to go by a different name, follow the customs of a new and strange religion, and invent a completely different history and background for yourself. If you fail to follow the "script" for this new life, you could face death. That's exactly what many young Jewish children had to do in order to stay alive in hiding.

Cécile Rojer was eleven years old when she was separated from her parents and sent to live in a convent in the Flemish part of Belgium. She was lucky that the nuns treated her well, but still she missed her parents desperately and once said, "Especially at night, I was sad remembering how my parents had been ripped away from me. Sometimes I cried myself to sleep, and I started wetting my bed."[4]

Only a small percentage of children were reunited with their parents after the war ended in 1945. While many children survived in hiding, their parents had died or been killed. The end of the war brought little happiness to these Jewish children who had been separated from their families. They were alive, but alone, with only memories of parents and siblings to comfort them.

---

[4] Rosenberg, Maxine. *Hiding to Survive: Stories of Jewish children rescued from the Holocaust*, p.57, New York: Clarion Books, 1994.

As you read the following stories about families who were separated from one another, try to imagine what your life would be like if you were all alone, apart from your family, and hiding to stay alive.

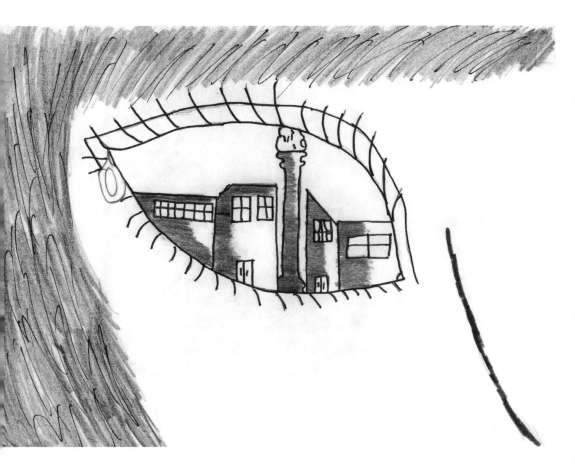

Thomas Wesley, Gr.7
Regina Mundi Catholic School, Hamilton, Ontario

Tonya Beliak

1942

My world has fallen apart in the past few weeks. There are rumors that we will either be killed in concentration camps, or forced to work there in brutal conditions. Many of us have been forced into hiding. People are doing anything to save their children. I have heard of people hiding under floor boards and not even speaking for fear of being caught.

My parents have been sent away. They knew of a German family that was willing to take me in and care for me as one of their own. The Mueller family are putting themselves at risk to protect me. Without them I would not be telling my story. I have to wear their son's clothes so I fit in.

Yesterday was a very scary day. I was playing in the living room with Lukas, the Mueller's son, when I heard a knock at the door. Mrs. Mueller answered it and my heart sank when I recognized the uniform of a Nazi officer. Mrs. Mueller was forced to let him in, and she and her husband were asked if they knew of any Jews that were hiding. They said no. When the soldier noticed me and came towards me, I said, *"Möchten sei einen tee, mein Herr?"* ("Would you like some tea, sir?") My question seemed to please the soldier and he stayed for a cup of tea. I was scared the entire time he was in the Mueller's home, worried I would be taken like so many Jews before me. I was grateful my parents had taught me some German and I know that my life was saved with those few words.

I fear for my parents and hope we will be reunited. I cannot imagine the future, but I must not forget the past. Still, I will carry on with my life. I can be sure of only one thing. It will not be easy.

This is a true story of Tonya Beliak, whose parents were killed in Auschwitz. Tonya is now married to Richard Beliak. They happily live in Fenelon Falls, Ontario, Canada. I have known Tonya for as long as I can remember as she lives next to my grandparents. I did not know of Tonya's past until recently. It is shocking how one group could succeed in discriminating against a religion so completely. I cannot get over the fact that someone I personally know has been through such an experience. I am amazed at the mental strength that Tonya and all the Jews who lived through the Holocaust have. I now see Tonya in a whole new way. Although she is a frail, elderly lady, she has a huge amount of courage and strength.[5]

William Hume, Gr.7
Eagle Ridge Public School, Ajax, Ontario

Child of the Holocaust

One of my favorite books about the Holocaust was *Child of the Holocaust*[iii] by Jack Kuper. Jankele Kuperblum was a nine-year-old Jewish boy who lived and worked on a farm in Poland during the early years of World War II. His real family lived in a nearby village, but he went to the farm to earn money to help them. Returning home for a visit, he discovered that the Nazis had rounded up all the Jews the night before. Jankele's farm family, the Pejzaks, changed his name to Kubus to hide his Jewish identity, but an older Pejzak brother, a Nazi sympathizer, insisted that he

---

[5] Sadly, Tonya Beliak passed away in December 2011, during the making of this book.

leave. He knew he had to forget his language, conceal his religion, and travel from town to town, and from shelter to shelter.

Jankele narrowly escaped some near-death experiences. At one point he had to hide in a cellar when the German soldiers inspected a farm he was staying on. He could hear the Germans walking in the field and was terrified as they got closer and closer. He could see them through the cracks in the cellar door, but luckily they could not see him. At another point, Jankele found himself in a field, with a German tank on one side exchanging fire with a tank from the Russian army.

Most of the families he met welcomed him, and he would make up stories about who he was and what had become of his own family. Some were aware that he was Jewish. Many wanted to protect him, but some, once they knew the truth, would ask that he leave in fear of what the Nazis would do to them. Jankele even begged a priest to convert him to Christianity, though the priest refused.

This book had a very strong impact on me. It revealed many details about the hardships during the war. It's interesting to know that the author is my friend's grandfather. When my friend came up to me in the library two years ago, holding that book, I wasn't sure I would be interested in reading it. I had not read many books about the Holocaust, but I thought I'd give it a chance, and I'm glad I did. I've even met the author several times. I find it amazing that this dignified, calm, and confident man was once a scared, little boy. Previously, the Holocaust was for me only a series of images and stories. But knowing Jack Kuper makes the story of the Holocaust so much more real.

Kate Hull, Gr.7
Glenview Senior Public School, Toronto, Ontario

Alone in the Ghetto

January 25th, 1944

Dear Diary,

Life here in the ghetto is getting worse; the strong are getting weak, and the weak are dying. The last of my family is now gone; my dear daughter, Leah, died a few nights ago. It was a cold and bitter night. All you could hear was the wind and the cries of the people. She fell asleep, but did not wake up in the morning. "Good night, Papa. I love you," were her last words and I will remember them forever.

I don't know if I can go on much longer. When my two wonderful children and loving wife were with me, it seemed like there was a reason to be strong and not give up. But this small room is closing in on me and the words that my beloved wife, Anna, whispered as she lay dying in my arms, "Promise me, Jacob, promise that you will stay strong, stay brave, and not die," are fading.

Still those few words are the only things holding me back from running out into the courtyard and calling to the Nazis, "Shoot me." I never broke a promise to my wife and I will try to keep this one.

As I sit on the floor of this barren room alone, I think of my life before all of this misery happened. I was a successful businessman providing for my family, living a good life. The wonderful, mouth-watering meals that Anna made are a distant memory. My oldest child, Chaim, who did not live past eleven, loved sports so much he would sleep in his uniform and make me play soccer with him every day after work. Leah, my youngest and bravest child, who was only eight when she passed from this earth, would go outside and come back in with a frog in the palm of her hand, her beautiful dress covered in mud, asking, "Can we keep him?" Every time I would answer her, "No, darling. He has a family of his own and they would miss him." I yearn for those days and that life. Our world has turned, and now you can be shot for buying bread or helping a stranger lying in the street.

A few days ago the Nazis took away thousands of people in trucks. We have no idea where they are going and if they will return. The rumors are that we will all die one way or another. My heart sank when I saw all of those trucks leave the ghetto. I shed a few tears and I walked along the empty streets with no one to keep me company except for a few bodies covered with newspaper.

This will also be my last entry from the ghetto, because as I write I have decided to escape, not just the ghetto but Poland, too. I am thinking of America. It sounds good there. It will be a new start. I don't know how I will do it, but I will find a way. If I die, at least I die trying.

Rachelle Wenting, Gr.8
Eugene Reimer Middle School, Abbotsford, British Columbia

Caught

I wish I could feel the warm sun and the fresh air again.

My whole family is hiding in our neighbor's cellar because the Nazis want to kill all the Jews. It is very cold and dark down here. Our neighbors are very kind and they always come down and give us food, but it is never enough for me and my whole family. We all try our best to make no noise. We have been hiding for days, weeks, and months. I fear that we will be killed.

One day, when I was heading over to the toilet, I stumbled and fell. I knew that I had broken my hand. Our neighbors tried their best to find a Jewish doctor, but they couldn't. Now, I can't move my hand anymore.

I hear Mama discuss with Papa that we need to be more careful because more and more soldiers are coming to inspect the house we are all hiding in. I am frightened!

The next day, there are footsteps upstairs. I am terrified by the noise. And that very moment, the thing I dread the most comes true: WE ARE CAUGHT!!!

They take us to a horrible place! As soon as we arrive, Mama and I are separated from the rest of my family. The guards patrol everywhere and the dogs bark loudly. This place is unimaginable, even in my worst dreams. Everyone is sick and hungry. I hope that someone rescues us, but all we do is wait. Mama gets sick the next week. She has a high fever and coughs a lot. We shout and scream for the soldiers to help us, but they don't. They come in and show us a gun. My mother becomes sicker. Next day, she doesn't open her eyes. Her body grows colder and colder.

Her heartbeat becomes slower and slower, and eventually everything in her body stops working. She dies.

One day, I wake up and don't see the guards or hear the dogs bark. In the midst of the silence I can hear heavy footsteps coming closer. The soldiers who enter the barrack are different. I learn later that they are the Allied forces. They are here to save us.

Kavya Patel, Gr.6
Williamsburg Public School, Whitby, Ontario

Please Help Me

August, 1941

Dear Journal,

I cannot stand living in this dreadful "camp." I have been here for two years. Living amongst death, starvation, and disease is worse than anyone could ever imagine. I wish it was over. Why is this my life?

Before I ended up in this camp, I was scared to death every day. I was waiting for the soldiers to come and tell my parents to leave our house. No one knew where people had gone or when they would return. Some of my friends would tell me that people from their family were sent away, and it devastated everyone. I felt lucky that it hadn't happened to my family yet. I would be sad if my grandparents, aunts, uncles, or cousins were taken away. What I didn't know was how devastated I would feel when my parents were the ones who were taken.

The night I heard someone knock on our door, I was scared. I was lying in my bed, just about to fall asleep. The noise made me jump and

I sat bolt upright. My heart was racing. I wondered who it was, but deep down, I think I knew. Who would come at eleven o'clock at night banging on the door? It was the soldiers.

I tried to look through the small crack behind the door. I wanted to see who was there. At first I wondered if it might be my aunt and uncle. It had been so long since I had seen them. But no. They lived too far away. Suddenly, I heard my mother screaming, something she never did. I knew something horrible must be happening. I hid behind our couch. My legs were shaking. My mother and father looked frightened. Now I was really scared. They didn't see me hiding behind the couch. It's a place I used to hide late at night, listening to my parents talk, or reading a book. My parents never seemed to notice me there.

I poked my head from behind, and saw the two men at the door. One was short and big around the waist and the other, tall and thin. They looked angry, standing in our doorway across from my parents. The soldiers had barged into our house without permission, and now these two creepy, silent men were walking around, looking at everything. They didn't seem to care that it wasn't their property.

When they were done, they started talking to each other. I could hear their German accent and their harsh voices, sounding as if they were scolding someone. And then, in a blink of an eye, they were gone and my parents were gone too. I didn't get to give them a good-bye hug or utter the words, "I love you." I watched them walk away in the soldiers' grip with tears in my eyes. My voice was silent, but my face was wet. In the days to follow, I sat in my house alone. No one came to get me. Over and over again, I asked myself these questions. Where had my parents gone?

What were they doing now? Why had they been taken away?

Eventually I too was arrested. But even after I was put into a concentration camp, I never found out what happened to my parents. To this day, I still don't know. I still ask myself those questions every night. I wonder if my parents are alive. I hope that they are not suffering. I hope that I will be reunited with them soon. Someone, please help me.

Zipporah Hruby, Gr.8
B'nai Shalom Day School, Greensboro, North Carolina

"I Just Want My Family"

The date is March 12, 1940. My name is Isaac Zebchynski. A year ago, we were forced into hiding. Sadly, we were caught, and now we have been placed in this railcar. I'm not quite sure where it's going to take us, but I know it won't be good, although right now, it seems like anywhere else would be better than right here.

My life before Hitler came into power was perfect. I come from a loving family of four. I'm only fifteen years old and it looks like my life isn't going to be perfect from now on, not even close. I hate to feel sorry for myself when I think of my little brother; he's only ten. Before Hitler forced all this hatred upon us, my mother cared for us at home. My father owned a string of restaurants throughout Germany, which was our main source of income. We weren't wealthy, but we did well.

But then the day came when Hitler announced all Jews would be arrested. A few days went by while we had to stay inside. We shut all the curtains and lay low for a while. We had to be cautious of Nazi soldiers barging in the house. On that day, February 26, 1940, we went upstairs to go to sleep in the small beds in the attic. After everyone else fell asleep I was still awake, and it scared me to be the only one who wasn't sleeping.

I could hear the sounds of army boots stomping around downstairs. I knew we were in for trouble and that there was nothing I could do, so I just tried to stay still. I heard the door to the attic burst open. Everyone else woke up. I held my breath and shut my eyes. They had captured us. We were arrested, put in a truck, and driven to holding cells in a bombed-out building.

After a few days, we were told that we would be leaving. At that moment we didn't know if we were going to be free or if we were just being moved to another cell. The soldiers took us and put us right back on a truck and started to drive us away. I was still confused and not sure what to think. After twenty minutes of driving it looked like we were coming to a stop. We pulled up to a rail station where there were hundreds, maybe thousands of Jewish people all crowded together, all looking as confused as I was.

A voice over a speaker ordered us to board the railcars. If I resisted, I knew I'd be shot. I stuck close to my mother, father, and brother, and we all boarded the railcar together. I could see my mother crying and I wished I could do something to end this horror.

We were on that railcar for three days, but it felt like forever. Everyone around us looked scared; some were crying, some screaming, some moaning, some dead. We had nothing to drink and nothing to eat. Mixed feelings between wanting to escape and wanting to stay with my family haunted me for the entire journey. By the end of those three days, just as I felt like dying, the doors of the railcar opened and a burst of light poured in.

A few people immediately ran out and they were shot. The shrieks and cries that followed were terrible. My family was so shocked after witnessing the shooting that we all hugged and stayed close together. Two Nazi soldiers then came up to our railcar. They signalled us to get out. They also had guns pointed towards us, so we did as we were told.

We walked out of the railcar and saw a huge building with smoke coming out of the chimney. There was a man in uniform who was directing people to one side of the train track or the other. It was a terrible scene because he was splitting up mothers and their children, brothers and sisters. If they refused, the man would signal Nazi soldiers over with guns. If they still refused, they would be shot. My family was split up. My father and I were sent to one side, and my mother and little brother were sent to the other.

It has now been two days since I have been separated from my mother and brother. We work all day long and are barely fed. The smell around this place is horrid. I don't really know what is going to happen next. I just hope I'll get to see the rest of my family. If I don't make it out of here, I just want people to know what we had to go through.

Isaac Robinson, Gr.8
Monsignor Morrison Catholic School, St. Thomas, Ontario

The Only One Left

Anne-Laure had always tried to forget what happened. The awful memories poisoned her mind, but she knew that telling her Canadian grandchild, Hanna, the truth of her past would help her recover for the future. As she sat across from Hanna, she began to talk.

"My family and I lived in Nantes, France when the war started. Thousands of Jewish people lost everything and I was one of them. When the Nazis took my parents, my elder sister, Claire, became my mother. For a while we were alone.

"I have to be grateful that my neighbors, Mr. and Mrs. Roi, took us in because life was better with them. We received healthy meals, and once a week we were allowed to walk around their garden, under the cover of night. After a month in their attic, Mrs. Roi told us that the French Resistance had arranged safe passage for Jews to escape from the country, and that the boat was leaving the next day. Claire promised me a better life, but it cost her hers."

Anne-Laure stopped, and tears were coming from her eyes. The memories were too painful. She remembered every detail, every sound of the horrible events that took place that night in France. Hanna took her hand and urged her to go on.

"The next day, only about an hour away from the departure time, someone came to the house. My sister and I froze in fear. Mrs. Roi answered the door, greeted the strange visitors, and led them to the kitchen. As they walked onto the floor, we heard the echo of their thick, leather soles. We knew who was paying us a visit. The Nazis were searching the house. Claire and I could only listen to them move further inside.

"We moved as quietly as possible to reach the door, but with the age of the house, every step caused the floorboards to creak. The voices downstairs hushed and Mrs. Roi tried to stall, but unsuccessfully.

"'Time to go,' Claire whispered and we rushed down the stairs and out the door. We ran down the street as screams followed us, and then, two clear gunshots.

"Claire pulled me into an alley. We did not speak for we were breathing hard, bent over from exhaustion. Then all too soon, Claire grabbed me by the hand and we continued sprinting, this time, with the Nazi officers racing at our heels. Twisting through the winding streets of Nantes, we took a sharp right and the harbor was in sight. But the boat on which we were meant to make our escape was already gone and pumping down the river.

"'We have to get to the bridge!' Claire gasped. She was right. The bridge was just low enough for us to jump onto the ship. We ran parallel to the right of the river and made a sharp left onto the bridge. The soldiers who were still on our heels screamed with rage as they figured out our plan. We reached the center of the bridge, right where the boat would pass and wasted no time climbing over the rail. When I jumped, I felt Claire's hand slip from mine. I landed hard on my knees and my vision was blurred with pain. I waited for Claire to join me, but she never did. The Nazi soldiers had caught her and were struggling to pull her back over the rail. I saw one officer leaning over the rail, yelling in frustration as he aimed his gun at me.

"The next few seconds seemed to happen almost in slow motion. As I raised my arms to protect my face from the oncoming bullet, I saw

Claire tackle the officer over the rail. He thrashed his arms to get a hold of something and caught Claire, dragging her over the rail with him. As I screamed her name, her body sank under the murky water. Then the world went black.

"I woke up days later in the ship, under the care of a woman named Gabriella. But I was ungrateful and selfish. I wanted Claire back. I was hysterical with grief, not believing that Claire was gone."

Anne-Laure's voice cracked at the last few words, and then she burst into tears, sobbing for what seemed like forever. She cried for her dead parents, her neighbors, and her sister who died protecting her. Hanna held her close and never let go.

Rachel McCarthy, Gr.7
Saint Margaret Mary Catholic School, Hamilton, Ontario

Chapter 3

Where Will We Hide?

Those Jewish families who were able to stay together still faced the extreme difficulty of finding a safe place to hide. Where to go? Who to turn to? Who to trust? Some people demanded a lot of money to hide Jewish families, something that few Jews at the time had.

One of the most well-known families who hid during the Holocaust was the family of Anne Frank. Anne was thirteen years old in 1942 when Margot, Anne's sister, received a summons from the SS. The family, fearing that Margot would be sent to a concentration camp, knew that they had to go into hiding. They were lucky that they had already found a place to hide, the attic of the building where Leo Frank, Anne's father worked. This place became known as "The Secret Annex." In one of the early entries in her diary, Anne wrote, "I can't tell you how oppressive it is never to be able to go outdoors, also I am very afraid that we will be discovered and shot." (September 28, 1942)

In the end, we know that Anne's family was eventually discovered and sent to the concentration camps. Anne and Margot died in Bergen-Belsen in March 1945, just months before the end of the war.

While Anne's story has been read by millions of young people, there are also thousands of stories of others who also hid with their families during the war. Some hid in barns or in the basements of homes owned by Christians who were willing to risk their lives for these Jews on the run. Some hid in the forests surrounding their towns or cities. Some, like Anne, hid in attics or areas of homes that were somehow concealed from the outside.

Born in Radom, Poland, Richard Rozen was only six years old when he hid with his parents in the home of a Christian family. Here's what he wrote about that time:

"I don't know how the contact was arranged, but there we stayed in what was actually a cabinet…My parents couldn't stand, but I could, and I sort of walked between them. This cabinet was in a cellar, so it was well-hidden. Our presence there was so secret, not even the children of the hiding family knew that we were there. That was where we stayed for thirteen months!"[6]

It's an understatement to say that hiding was a terrifying time for Jewish families. They had little food to eat, nothing to do all day long, nowhere to run or play; they faced illness with no medicine, and the constant fear that they would be discovered. Here are some stories about families who managed to hide together. Those who did survive this way count themselves among the lucky ones.

---

[6] www.history1900s.about.com/od/holocaust/a/hiddenchildren

On the Run

November 29th, 1941

Dear Diary,

I cannot do this anymore! The war has to stop. My life cannot be based on hiding from the Nazis and keeping away from concentration camps! We need to be free; I cannot bear this life anymore.

This morning was a close call; Jacob, Eric, and I were almost caught. When Mrs. Enga, the owner of the house that we were hiding in, opened the door to the Gestapo, they demanded that she reveal any Jewish people hiding in her house. Mrs. Enga simply lied to the Gestapo, telling them, "I have no intention of disobeying the law and would not hide a Jew." Believing her, the Gestapo left.

Then Jacob spoke aloud, not noticing the Gestapo were still outside the house. "They believed you!" he exclaimed in amazement. At that moment I knew all three of us were in trouble. I saw the Gestapo catch a glimpse of Jacob and they came rushing in to capture us! As the Gestapo came into the house, Mrs. Enga yelled to me, "Anna, run! And take care of your brothers!"

I grabbed Jacob's and Eric's trembling hands and barged out the back door, dragging my brothers behind me. With my heart beating a thousand times a minute and the Gestapo ordering us to stop, I managed to lead Eric and Jacob into the woods until the Gestapo got a hand on Jacob! They must have done something horrible to him. I heard him scream from the pain. Eric forced me to keep on running, but I felt like falling down on the ground and breaking into tears. Then I heard it, the sound I dreaded – a gunshot! My legs felt like jelly, but Eric kept me running.

I do not feel the need for my life to continue, but I know I have to for Eric. My family was complete five years ago, with two loving parents, Eric, my ten-year-old brother, and Jacob who was eight. He was only eight! How could this have happened? He didn't deserve to die! Now my family is only my brother and me! I am a thirteen-year-old girl with no place to live and no safe place for me to raise my brother. I cannot give up though; I have to keep hope!

Sarah Eng, Gr.7
Glenview Senior Public School, Toronto, Ontario

Courage

Dear Anne Frank,

I can't imagine how hard it is to be locked up with no way out, but I can try to make it better. Read this and think of sunshine, the outside world, and the madness being over. You are so strong, and I wish I could meet you to learn from your immense courage. I was once told a quote that reminds me of you: "Courage is not the towering oak that sees storms come and go; it is the fragile blossom that opens in the snow."[iv] Always remember that you are a survivor and you are the type of person with whom the world should be filled. You are one of a kind, Anne, special and pure, and I wish we could meet and become great friends.

Shanice Pereira, Gr.8
Fieldstone Day School, Toronto, Ontario

Are You There?

Dear Diary,

My name is Abigail Gutenstof. I am twelve years old. I come from a large family. There are nine of us in total. I have five sisters and three brothers.

Mama and Papa met when they were teenagers and they fell in love and married right away. Life was great until not long ago. Now they have been fighting a lot since Rosa, my eldest sister, died, or should I say was killed by a Nazi soldier. You see, Adolf Hitler has come to power and we're in the midst of a war.

We are in hiding because we are Jewish. We are those whom Hitler's Nazi soldiers are looking for. Our race is being slowly slaughtered – an unbelievable crime – for being Jewish. Papa says we will be safer fleeing from our home and staying away.

Since the war started we have lost much: our home, our friends, and our family. Our grandparents were both ill and in hospital, until the order came to burn down the hospital and everyone inside it. We are always afraid that we will be found and sent away, sent to one of the concentration camps with their gas chambers that we have heard rumors about.

Mama and Papa always say that if we stay together and stay strong, this will all pass. The younger children believe this while the older ones, including me, have our doubts. I have prayed every night since the war started and still no answer. God, I have just one question! Are you really there? Or are you just sitting there watching us suffer? Please hear my prayers and take away the darkness that has fallen upon us. Please save us before the world catches fire from Hitler's madness, and do it soon, for all our sakes.

Olivia Difede, Gr.6
St. Wilfred Catholic School, Pickering, Ontario

Rose's Secret

"Rose! Sarah! Quick, girls! Run!" my mother called out to us. The house was burning to the ground around us. All I could do was pray that the Nazis wouldn't find me, my mother, and sister.

"Rose! I will meet you in our safe place!" Mama called after me. "Take Sarah with you!"

"Sarah, where are you?" I shouted. I heard quiet whimpering.

"Mama," a small voice sobbed.

"Sarah!" I exclaimed. "There you are! Come quick! We must go to the safe place!" I called to her over the noise of the flames.

We ran outside and reached our hiding place, a dark cellar that had been dug into the ground. It was sparsely furnished with a cupboard to hold our emergency supplies. I shut the trap door once we were safely inside and walked over to Sarah, handing her a blanket. We huddled in the dark corner of the cellar. Then I remembered the space I had dug beneath the supply cupboard. It was a secret hiding spot that not even Mama knew about.

I pushed the cupboard aside. "I knew this day would come," I explained to Sarah. "Come here."

Sarah walked slowly towards the secret opening. The ends of the blanket dragged behind her. She looked down into the darkness. "Jump into the hole. It is safer down there than up here," I told her just as my mother appeared in our cellar. My mother jumped next, saw that Sarah was fine, and held out her arms for me. I followed.

"I knew this day would come, and when it did we would need a shelter," I explained to my mother and sister. "I made this space while we were digging out the top area. We must remain down here until we know it is safe to go up. I have collected food and blankets, and some books," I added.

We remained safely hidden for some time. But when there were no supplies left, I knew we had to leave. We had to make a plan, and fast. We had to make it to the city. Some days we were able to sneak food from food carts in the streets there. It was a treacherous time, but we made it all in one piece, alive and together.

Meagan Hodgetts, Gr.6
Assumption School, Aylmer, Ontario

Anne Frank — A Profound Effect

Io ho letto un libro che mi ha colpito. E' il diario di Anna Frank, una bambina ebrea che quando compì 13 anni ricevette in dono un diario, dove scrisse tutto quello che le stava succedendo.

Benché la sua famiglia avesse cercato di nascondersi dai nazisti, nel retro dell'ufficio del padre i soldati arrivarono, li arrestarono e li portarono nei campi di concentramento.

Il campo di concentramento era un campo di lavoro dove si lavorava

duramente. Quando i prigionieri non facevano abbastanza venivano man-
dati alle camere a gas.

I nazisti toglievano la vita agli altri. Io penso che siamo tutti uguali e
che non c'è senso a perseguitare e a far male ad altri esseri umani.

I read a book that moved me. It is *The Diary of Anne Frank*, in which a thirteen-year-old Jewish girl was given a diary where she wrote down everything that was going on in her life.

Even though her family tried to hide from the Nazis in the back office of her father's business, the soldiers arrived, arrested the people, and took them to concentration camps.

The concentration camp was a place to work and they did work hard. When the prisoners did not do enough, they were sent to the gas chambers.

The Nazis took the lives of others. I think we are all equal and it makes no sense to harass and hurt other human beings.

Samuele Fadda
Istituto Comprensivo Thiesi, Sardinia, Italy

A Letter to Otto Frank

Dear Mr. Otto Frank,

This year, I had the opportunity to go to Amsterdam and visit the Anne Frank house. I waited for an hour in the line up and while waiting, my mind went back to an earlier time when I first learned about the Holocaust. I was in grade five when we were asked to read a Holocaust novel. I knew in my head that these events were real, but I just could not bring myself to believe what hardship people lived through during this time period, and how much they suffered. I had a hard time understanding how it must have felt to live through such horror. After reading your daughter Anne's diary it became clearer to me how people were feeling in their day-to-day lives.

As I was standing in line that day in Amsterdam, I could not believe I was going into Anne's house. When I entered, my eyes were drawn to Anne's quotes on the walls of each room; it gave me a sense of what it was really like to go into hiding. "At the stroke of half past eight, he [her father] has to be in the living room. No running water, no flushing lavatory, no walking around, no noise whatsoever."[v] This quote from your daughter's diary made me realize that going into hiding at this time was not a game like hide-and-seek, but rather something that could determine your future. You needed to have a lot of will power in order to follow the rules. You could not just come out of hiding and say, "Here I am!"

I never fully understood freedom until I went to Anne's house and realized what it means to live without it. I saw the small space in which you lived and the blacked out windows. It all made sense why Anne would make the comment, "I feel like a bird in a cage."[vi] I cannot imagine what it must have been like for you and your family not to stand on green grass or smell fresh air – not to do the simple things that I take for granted. I do not know what I would do if I could not shout or run free. I admire Anne. She was able to look through the window and get the most from life just by watching the world, to write in her diary and let her thoughts out without screaming.

Anne was a real girl around my age, and what she was going through with her family at the time is more or less what I am going through with mine now. I can relate to her better than I can relate to an adult because she was becoming a teenager just like me.

Your daughter, Anne, has given me a different perspective on the Holocaust. She has put her feelings into words that I can comprehend. This has made the events of this time very real to me and helped me to understand what people were going through.

You might be asking yourself, "Why is this girl writing this letter to me?" Here is your answer. I am writing you this letter now, not because my teacher, mother, friends, or family told me to, but because my heart did. When I do something incredible, I like to know that people appreciate it, and I want you to know that I appreciate what you did. You went back to your horrifying past, to the house where the nameless happened, and turned it into a museum for the public to see. You might say, "How can one visit to a house answer so many questions?" But it did. I can now see who and what a true hero is, and you and your family are among them. You were able to live the unimaginable and then move forward. For that I would like to say thank you.

Rachel Meyerovitz, Gr.8
Robbins Hebrew Academy, Toronto, Ontario

Chapter 4

The Fear Is Overwhelming!

Have you ever been afraid? Of course you have. There isn't a person alive that hasn't faced a fear of some kind. Whether it's going to the dentist, or flying in a plane, or watching a scary movie, or being in a lightning storm, we have all experienced a time when our hearts beat faster, our breath quickened, and we counted the seconds for that terrifying moment to end. And for most of us, the frightening event eventually passed and we went on with our lives.

Now, imagine what it would be like to live in that terrifying state for months, or even years! That's the reality that most Jewish families faced during the Holocaust. Fear was constant. It was the state you woke up with and it stayed with you long into the night.

Perhaps nowhere was the fear greater than inside the concentration camps. The circumstances there were truly horrific. Jewish prisoners were starved and made to work under unbearably harsh conditions. They were exposed to the cold of winter with little clothing to protect them. They contracted diseases such as typhus and had no medication to cure them. They were beaten and tortured on a regular basis. One wrong step or one look from a Nazi guard could get you shot on the spot. The terror was intense and it was relentless.

"I lived in such fear. I experienced such evilness."[7] Helen Sternlicht, a Polish Jewish teenager, once said that as she recalled her experience of being imprisoned in the Plaszow concentration camp. There, she was made to work as a maid for the camp commander, Amon Goeth. He was a madman who was known to brutalize the Jewish prisoners. He carried a rifle and would randomly shoot out the window at prisoners who worked below. Though her parents perished, Helen and her two sisters were rescued by Oskar Schindler, a German businessman who saved the lives of over one thousand Jews by employing them in factories. His life was made famous in the Steven Spielberg film, *Schindler's List*.[8]

In this chapter, students have written stories reflecting the terror that Jews experienced at that time. Fear was a by-product of this war, and Jews felt it all the time.

---

[7] Helen Sternlicht, The Palm Beach Post News, www.palmbeachpost.com/news
[8] *Schindler's List*. Dir. Steven Spielberg, Perf. Liam Neeson, Ralph Fiennes, Ben Kingsley. Universal Pictures, 1993.

The Unknown Truth

Snuggling close to her mother, Leah shivered as the train raced through the gloomy fog. The distinct chill in the air was a sign of the impending winter. Now she was on a train, as the Nazis had ordered, bound for the unknown.

Only three days ago, Leah and her family, along with all the Jews of the community, had been ordered to pack their belongings. Life in this town had been peaceful, but now fear had set in like a heavy looming storm. Questions had been flying everywhere as people talked nervously. *Where are we going? What should we take? Is it safe where we are going? What will become of us? Will we ever come back?*

"Mama, I'm scared," whispered Leah into her mother's ear, making sure they never lost contact with each other. The train was filled to the brim. People were squashed close to one another like sardines packed together inside a can. Leah could feel her father's warm breath blowing into her ear as he sat pressed between Leah and the carriage wall.

After what seemed like days, they finally disembarked to find Nazis standing there waiting for them in the rain. Then, everyone was ordered to march in a straight line. They marched and they marched, trudging closer to the ghetto, their new home. Leah cuddled up close to her mother as they walked on through the fierce wind.

The ghetto buildings stared down at them like kings of the world. Leah felt as if she was merely a grain in this desert of dread. Rats raced rapidly searching for food. The men were ordered to go to one building while the women were ordered to another. All the children were driven forward toward the barn that stood in the middle. Leah was heartbroken.

She was seven years old and was already waving good-bye to her parents.

It was then that Leah felt a soft, calming hand slide into hers. An older girl named Sara led Leah to the confines of the barn as Leah's eyes remained frozen on the gate that had slammed shut on her mother. Once inside, Leah crawled upon a thin mattress. Her eyes were alive again, but there was no light, just a dull and lonely glistening of tears.

Memories of previous Sabbath dinners with her parents flickered through her head like fireflies occasionally glowing. Leah knew that sitting at the dining table with her parents enjoying a family meal would be no more. She would never smell her mother's chicken soup boiling on the stove or hear the sweetness in her father's voice as he sang the evening prayers. She would never feel the warmth of her bedroom, scattered with her toys and treasures. She would never feel the comfort of her family again.

Just then, Leah felt a hand on her shoulder. Through glazed eyes, she looked up to find herself staring into the deep, dark eyes of a guard.

Becki Friderich, Gr.6
Captain Woollahra Public School, New South Wales, Australia

Everything Goes Black

I had the dream again, the same one I've had every night since I've been hiding in the cellar of this abandoned house. In my dream, it is 1935 and I am only five years old. But for some reason, I can remember every detail about my life back when it was perfect, back when it didn't matter that you were Jewish. I am playing jump rope and hopscotch with my friends, Ava, Elsbeth, Kurt, and Abraham. We are laughing at the boys trying to jump rope, but getting caught in it instead, and tripping over themselves, falling onto the ground. We are all so happy and I am laughing so hard there is a pain in my stomach. But then we all stop abruptly when we see who is advancing towards us.

Marching down the sidewalk in long orderly strides are two tall men dressed in black pants and shirts that are muddy brown. The brown shirts have a red band around the arm with a symbol on it that looks somewhat like the letter X. They wear black caps upon their heads and heavy-looking boots on their feet that make a loud *THUD* as they strut down the sidewalk.

My dream is rudely interrupted by the sound of men screaming at me. My eyes open quickly, and in front of my face I see a pair of dark black shiny boots. Nausea spreads to my stomach as I look up and see three Nazis standing over me, two with their hands on their guns. The one right in front of me is very tall, and he has eyes as blue as the ocean. I can see dirty blond hair coming out from his cap – "the perfect Aryan," I think. He yells "Up!" at me, but I am too scared to move. I can see the little patience he has in eyes is wearing thin. My mind is telling me to move, but my body won't budge. He grabs a fistful of my hair and I yelp in pain. He drags me up to my feet, muttering, "Filthy Jew." The Nazi soldier leads me outside, a place I haven't seen in years.

When I am outside it is terribly bright, and there are four more Nazi soldiers. They escort me onto a train crammed with hundreds of other Jews. Everywhere around me, people are crying and screaming, most of them looking sickly. It smells awful on the train. But nothing can prepare me for what I see when I step off. There are no words to describe the scene; I fight the urge to vomit. Groups of Jews are being herded off the trains by Nazi soldiers pointing guns in their faces. Those who fall are beaten, badly. I see one little boy, no older than six, gripping his father's pants for dear life, his face as pale as stone.

The Nazis order us to get into two separate lines: women on one side, men on the other. The elderly, sickly looking adults and children are sent to the left, while most men and healthy looking people are sent to the right. I finally reach the front of the line after what seems like hours. There is a man there who decides where everyone goes. He looks at me and then sends me to the left.

My heart is pounding. I pray that this line leads to somewhere safe. But the soldiers are leading me and hundreds of Jews to a building. The smell back here is so much worse than it was in the front, and people around me are gagging. They cram us all in a small room with barely enough room to breathe and order us to take off our clothes so we can have a shower. Why are they suddenly starting to treat us nicely? After everyone has taken off their clothes, they rush us into a bigger room that is pitch black, and they lock us in.

Women are screaming, children are crying, and everything is chaotic. Suddenly, my nose, throat, and eyes start to burn, and I smell something strange in the air that hasn't been there before. It is getting harder to breathe, the screaming is coming to a stop, and then everything goes black…

Mykaela Officer, Gr.7
Eagle Ridge Public School, Ajax, Ontario

The Holocaust Through the Eyes of Hana Brady

October 21, 1944

I am going to see George again! Ever since he left in September, I have not written in this book and I have been lonelier than ever. I miss him terribly and I am really on my own, now. My mother is gone, my father is gone, and my grandmother is gone, too. Now, even my brother is gone. Since he left, I have not talked to too many of the other girls. Ella has been the exception. I know she has tried to comfort me, but none of it has worked.

But when I saw my name on the list of those who would be sent to the railroad tracks, my heart was filled with joy! I will see George again and I want to look my best for him. I want to show him just how well I have been taking care of myself. Ella is helping me to do this. She has cleaned me up and made me feel good inside. I will always be grateful to her.

As the girls quiet down on the train, I hear angry voices, and suddenly I realize what is happening. The voices are too rough and deep to belong to any of the girls. It is Nazi soldiers. Now I wonder where we are going, what will happen to us, and whether I will really see George. I do not know what the Nazis are talking about, but I hope it is not about us.

October 22, 1944

My stomach is rumbling. Ella, the others, and I are starving. There is no food on this train and we have been on it for a long time. To make matters worse, there is no water here either! Plus, no toilet! Some of the girls found some buckets, but I am not using those. Without eating or drinking anything, I have not had to relieve myself. Yesterday, I was too excited about seeing George to even worry about food. Now my thirst and hunger are catching up to me. Who knows how much longer we will have to be in this death trap. Most of the girls around me are much too weak to move!

October 23, 1944

We have arrived at some awful place. We need water! I hear more talking coming from the Nazis, but I still cannot understand what they are saying.

Nazis are everywhere. They have ordered the taller and older girls to go in another direction. At least I have Ella. They are directing us to go somewhere now. I wonder if George will be there. I hope so! Ella is telling me to follow her.

We were at the front of the line, so we arrive first. We are now in a large building, and still no George. There are many more girls coming in. I wonder what will happen to us. I hope we will be all right. As I see all of my friends' faces, I become even more nervous. Their eyes show the same thing – fear. I am sure that they can all see it on my face, too.

All of the girls are inside. The doors are shut. What is happening?

Hana Brady died in the gas chambers of Auschwitz at the age of thirteen. Many Jews faced what she had to face. But a lucky few lived and were sent to work. George Brady, Hana's brother was one of them. He is still alive today and talks to many others about Hitler and the Holocaust through the story of Hana's Suitcase.[vii]

Eftiola Sholla, Gr.7
Regina Mundi Catholic School, Hamilton, Ontario

Hannah Feldman, Gr.6A
Downtown Jewish Community School, Toronto, Ontario

The Cattle Car

In preparation for my Bar Mitzvah, I participated in a "twinning" program in Toronto, in order to show my respect for the 1.5 million children who were murdered during the Holocaust. This fictional short story is inspired by, and dedicated to, the memory of my twin, Yona.

In the spring of 1942, a cattle car rushes past a lush forest in southern Poland, a forest rich with the beauty of Eastern Europe. The sky shines a brilliant blue across both the tops of century-old trees and the petals of week-old flowers – the contrast between the two is acknowledged by an eleven-year-old boy pressed against a gap between the wooden slats of the car. He peers out at the trees with passivity, but at the flowers with focussed, blissful concentration. The boy also acknowledges the devastating dissimilarity between life outside the car and life on the inside. As he turns his head toward the interior of the cattle car in which he is entrapped, he notices a newborn baby girl at his feet, and senses the irrefutable, overwhelming anxiety of her mother. He also witnesses an elderly man sitting on the floor, in addition to a middle-aged woman, whom he recognizes instantly as a co-worker of his father. Panic, he concludes, is a consistent emotion amongst this group of people. However, even though the boy is empathetic and considerate, he needs to maintain an emotional distance between himself and the rest of his community; he knows himself, knows that he is sensitive and easily unsettled by the feelings of others.

Nonetheless, he feels nervous about where he is being taken, a realization that ever since Hitler became the leader of Germany, life has changed. Non-Jewish people from his town have become more disgruntled – angrier, edgier. The eleven-year-old boy seems to understand that people, by nature, feel more confident when they blame failures on other groups of people – in this case, Jews – so he knows exactly why he has been treated so unfairly. He knows why he was humiliatingly singled out as he wore a yellow *Magen David* on his clothing. He knows why he was expelled from school. He knows why he couldn't play outside his home after seven o'clock in the evening. Oddly, he finds it intriguing that the situation he was in was a result of human nature in action, demonstrating its baser instincts. More than that, the boy grasps that he was an integral part of something bigger than himself, even though it did hurt to be singled out in his town. It hurt to be perceived as racially inferior to those around him. And he seems to know that the human race will remember this time as an era during which people were hurt very badly.

Suddenly, a jolt brings the boy back to reality, crushed against the wall of the cattle car. He hears crying and moaning, and the expressions of many people around him are making him feel frightened and confused. He wonders if he will ever see his parents again.

A cattle car passes the lush forest in Poland, in 1942. A harsh breeze sways young, vibrant flowers towards old, dark trees under the sky's brilliant blue, as a storm brews overhead. A farmer watches from a comfortable distance, waiting for the weather to take its toll.

Benjamin Feldman, Gr.8
Downtown Jewish Community School, Toronto, Ontario

Chapter 5

The Goodness of Some

"Righteous Among the Nations" is the phrase used to describe those non-Jewish individuals who were willing to risk their lives to help Jewish people during the Holocaust. It took an incredibly compassionate and brave person to reach out to his or her Jewish neighbor and extend a helping hand. The punishments for defying Nazi orders and helping Jews were severe. Those who helped Jews could be arrested, deported to prison camps, shot on the spot, or publicly hanged. The Nazis wanted to make sure that everyone understood the danger of breaking their rules. And yet, there were some who were willing to take their chances and did just that. These are the people who hid Jews in their homes, or smuggled Jewish children out of ghettos, or refused to be pressured into turning over their Jewish neighbors to the Nazis. Sadly, there were not enough of these brave individuals at that time. Had more people been willing to stand up to the Nazis and protect more Jews, the outcome of this time in history would have been significantly different.

In this chapter's stories, you will discover famous heroes such as Irena Sendler and others who have been named "Righteous Among the Nations" for helping Jews during the Holocaust. You will also read about several less famous people who were equally courageous.

As you read the following stories of those individuals who defied the rules and their own fears in order to help others, ask yourself: What would I be willing to do in a dangerous situation? Would I be able to ignore someone who is suffering or being treated unjustly? What if I might face consequences for helping someone in need?

It's impossible to know what any one of us might do in these circumstances. But be inspired by those who stood apart from the crowd, who risked their own safety, who tried to make a difference in the outcome of the Holocaust by helping others.

The Boy Who Sat Beside Me

In school my history teacher was trying to teach us about the Holocaust. How were we supposed to learn anything from a bunch of books and websites? I wasn't there; I don't know what it was like. To me learning about the Holocaust was going to be a long, boring journey. That was before a new kid came to our class.

Michael was of average height and a little on the bulky side. He had dark brown eyes that showed thoughtfulness and kindness.

My teacher asked me to be his guide. "I think you two will be great friends," she said. We shook hands.

Later in the day, I mentioned to Michael that we were studying the Holocaust and that I wasn't enthusiastic about that. Michael got really quiet. Eventually he said, "My great-grandparents were survivors of the Holocaust. They have told me stories of their time in Germany and how horrible it really was."

I thought for a minute and said, "I'm sorry, I had no idea. Maybe the reason I don't like learning about the Holocaust is because I can't relate to it. If you want, you could tell me something about your great-grandparents."

Michael smiled and rummaged in his knapsack. He handed me a notebook and said, "Here is something I wrote…"

To Erik it was another day. He woke up in the morning to the sound of his mother's voice. Then he quietly dressed and went downstairs. After he had had breakfast, he walked to school, passing through "Devil's Road" on the way. It was called that because mostly Jewish people lived there, and Erik was taught in his Hitler Youth group that the Jewish people were to blame for all the problems around Germany. The street was still littered with shattered pieces of broken furniture and shards of glass, and some buildings were still smoking after *Kristallnacht*, a riot which had occurred a couple of nights before. Erik tried not to breathe in the hazy air around him or look at the broken stores and lost livelihood of the Jewish people.

He arrived at school and attended his classes. When he was returning home he walked through Devil's Road again. This time he was about halfway down the street when a young boy approached him. He grabbed Erik's arm, holding him in place. The boy's eyes were a dark brown and they looked too old for the face that carried them, as if the boy had seen too much. He said, "Please, do you have any food? My family is starving to death."

Erik was shocked. He didn't move or say anything. Finally he nodded and reached into his bag. There was still some food left over from his lunch. He handed over the scraps to the boy, who looked astounded, but gratefully took them and turned to go. Before he left, Erik called after him, "What's your name?"

The boy replied with a small smile on his face. "Chaim."

Later that night, Erik thought about that moment again. He remembered how the boy's shirt with the yellow star on the pocket was far too light for the cold wind that blew that day, and the way his ribs were sticking out a little too much under the shirt. Erik dwelled upon the realization that Chaim and he weren't all that different. But what he remembered most was the feeling he had inside him when he gave the food to the boy. It was a feeling of joy. Right then and there, Erik decided that he would help Chaim in any way he could.

Over the next few weeks, Erik brought food to Devil's Road. He was careful to walk past the street if there was a German patrol nearby. But he always went out of his way to talk to Chaim. The boys became friends. Erik learned that Chaim's father had been taken away on the night of *Kristallnacht* and that they hadn't heard from him since. Chaim also told Erik that he was afraid that he and his brother, Hershel, would also be arrested. Erik began to fear for his friend's life.

It had been a couple of months and Erik was delivering his daily small scraps of food. He had just given the last of the food away when a strong hand gripped his shoulder. He turned around slowly to face a man he vaguely knew. The man looked at Erik. He said, "Be more careful about helping. Watch the street and vary your patterns. Got it?"

Erik nodded silently and left. After this experience, he followed that man's advice and went on random days and at varying times. He knew that Chaim was no longer safe. There were too many bystanders watching, waiting to snitch, and too many soldiers ready to act. The time had come. He decided to tell Chaim that he should run.

The next day Erik visited Chaim's house, but no one was home. He discovered that soldiers had come the night before and taken the family away. Erik was horror-struck, but still determined to help his friend.

He decided to hide on one of the army trucks that passed through town. Erik didn't think about what would happen if he got caught. The next afternoon he packed extra food and clothes, enough for a three-day journey. He didn't tell his family where he was going. With his bag in tow, he spotted an army truck and silently made his way towards it.

A tarp was pulled over the back of the truck so all Erik had to do was look around and slip under. The next thing Erik knew, he was bouncing along a dirt road. The vehicle finally stopped after what seemed like days. Erik pulled himself up into a sitting position, dragged his numb body outside the truck, and looked around.

He was near a fenced-in area. There were thick steel wires that wrapped around tall wooden poles. If he squinted he could see log buildings that were lined up like rows of marching soldiers. Erik could hear the pounding of boots nearby and shouts from unknown mouths. Inside the fence were children huddling together for warmth. Their faces were innocent and young. Erik sneaked quietly out of the bushes and motioned for the children to come near.

One of the boys, the oldest, moved forward. "You shouldn't be here. You could get killed," he whispered.

Erik shook his head, "I'm here to find my friend. His name is Chaim, about my age."

The boy thought for a moment. Finally he replied, "I can bring him here. It'll take a few minutes so the guards don't get suspicious. Wait in the bushes."

When Chaim was in sight, Erik slithered out of the bushes to the edge of the fence. Chaim's eyes grew wide with disbelief when he saw his friend.

"What are you doing here? It isn't safe. Do you want to get killed?" Chaim's face had transformed from shock to outrage. "Please, if you are actually my friend, go home and never return."

"Is that really what you want?" asked Erik. Chaim said nothing and Erik continued, "Fine, but please take the food and give it to the others."

Chaim took the food that Erik pushed through the fence. Tears were forming in both boys' eyes. Who knew if they would see each other again? Erik nodded good-bye and then retreated into the forest.

Several days later, he stumbled home. He never told his family where he had been or even about Chaim. Erik continued to help those who were struggling around him in every way he could – giving scraps of food here, old clothing there.

When the war ended, Erik went in search of Chaim. He learned that Chaim had starved to death in the concentration camps. Erik never forgot his friendship with Chaim and carried the memory of him with him all his life.

After I read Michael's story I was shocked. How could such a horrible thing have happened to people who weren't all that different from me? Eventually I asked, "So how did this finish for your great-grandparents?"

"My great-grandfather was Chaim's little brother, Hershel. Chaim died because he was giving most of his food to Hershel. Hershel survived and then moved to the United States. Before Hershel moved, Erik found him and told him how his brother, Chaim, had changed his life. This story has been passed down in my family ever since."

The story made me realize that I can relate to the Holocaust in more ways than I ever thought.

Kathryn Tellian, Gr.8
MacGregor Public School, Waterloo, Ontario

Irena Sendler: A True Hero

Heroes are all around us. They perform actions and possess qualities that make them thought of and remembered as heroes. Irena Sendler chose to act heroically when many did not. She was reliable, brave, and modest. By possessing these qualities and acting on them, she became a hero, not just to the people she saved, but to their families and to those familiar with her story.

When she saved the lives of children, Irena did not have to deal just with the Polish police and the Nazis, she also had to deal with the children's parents. It was extremely difficult to ask a mother and father if she could take their child, even if it was to save that child's life. So Irena told these parents that she would keep track of every child she took. She filled jars with strips of paper with each child's real name, birth date, parental information, and hiding location. Irena planned to use this information to reunite families at a later date, or at least tell the hidden children the truth about their backgrounds. It was extremely hard for parents to believe in her, but it was the only choice they had. Irena kept her word and she was able to keep track of the more than 2,500 children she saved. She said, "Every child saved with my help is a justification of my existence on this earth; [I'm] not entitled to glory."[viii] She never thought of fame or glory in her work.

Irena knew that it was wrong to discriminate against Jews and decided to do something about it. On October 20, 1943, Irena was caught and was tortured. She was asked to reveal where she was hiding the children and who was helping her, but she did not give in. This only resulted in more torture. She was then sentenced to death, but luckily she was saved. Her courage while being tortured was yet another selfless action that put the fate of others before her own. "I was brought up to believe that a person must be rescued when drowning, regardless of religion and nationality."[ix] That is exactly what Irena did; she helped the people who were in need in the ghettos.

Irena never went public with her heroic deeds until she was much older. Saving people and knowing they were saved was good enough for her. She just felt that what she did was right. Looking back on her actions, Irena said, "Let me stress most emphatically that we who were rescuing children are not some kind of heroes. Indeed, that term irritates me greatly. The opposite is true. I continue to have pangs of conscience that I did so little."[x] This quote says a lot about Irena. In her opinion, helping people escape death was her duty.

Irena Sendler is truly special. Her acts of reliability, bravery, and modesty are what enabled her to save the lives of over 2,500 people. She will be remembered forever in the hearts of millions. Irena Sendler truly earns the right to be called a hero.

Adam Hoffman, Gr.7
Yorkhill Elementary School, Thornhill, Ontario

In Hiding

November 14, 1943

Winter is just around the corner. You can tell that the Nazis were here last night. Their boot marks are still imprinted in the snow.

It has been difficult with Father gone. Last month the Nazis took him to a concentration camp. Mother has to do everything alone. I have three sisters and four brothers. Luckily, Mother's good friend, Beatrice, has been stopping by to help.

However, that isn't our only trouble.

Our family is Jewish, and Nazi soldiers have been taking Jews away. Because of this, we are in hiding. Food has been rationed. There is no butter, sugar, or coffee. We are hiding in the basement of a bakery. There are two other Jews hiding here. The owner of the bakery has been very kind. Mother has been trying to repay him, but we have very little money. It is cramped and cold in here.

Two days ago we were all devastated to hear that our dear friend, Peter, died. He secretly fought the Nazis by helping Jews. He was caught and executed for trying to deliver Jews to Sweden,[9] where it is safe. My oldest brother is the most upset. He and Peter were very good friends. He will not speak to anyone.

I believe we will be moving to a larger hiding spot. The Nazis will soon figure out that we are here. They are inspecting all shops. My ink is running out. I must save it for another time.

Julia Vail, Gr.6
Hamburg Middle School, Hamburg, New York

---

[9] During the Second World War, Sweden remained a neutral country. Many Jews tried to escape there.

Saving a Life

In un film che ho visto intitolato Schindler's List *mi ha colpito molto una frase che viene detta dagli ebrei che vengono salvati da Oscar Schindler : "Salvare una persona è come salvare l'umanità intera." Ho capito che tutte le persone, che salvarono gli ebrei, erano generose e coraggiose perché per farlo rischiarono la vita.*

In a movie I saw called *Schindler's List*, I was very impressed with a statement that was made by the Jews who were saved by Oskar Schindler: "Whoever saves one life, saves the entire world." I realized that all the people who saved Jews were generous and courageous because they risked their lives to do it.

Rosa Canu
Istituto Comprensivo Thiesi, Sardinia, Italy

More than Just Facts

Last year, my parents took me to listen to a Holocaust survivor speak. As he started talking, I soon realized that this was no ordinary experience. He spoke with great expression. At times, he would shout, displaying both fear and disgust. The speaker was not only very knowledgeable about the Holocaust, he was exceptional at telling his story.

The story began when he was eleven and his sister was seven years old. His family was about to be taken to the Auschwitz concentration camp. His parents told him to run away as fast and as far as he could toward the border, and that a relative would be waiting for him there.

He set off running with his sister. He ran and ran until total exhaustion overcame him. He and his sister did not have water, food or shelter. As night fell, they came to a farm and decided to hide in the barn with the horses, sheep, and a dog. Every morning, the farmer would come into the barn and fill the animals' food trays. The children would take a portion of the dog's food and water to stay alive. They lived like this for three weeks, until the farmer found them. The farmer did not say a word and walked out of the barn. The next morning, the farmer brought in two additional trays of food. The children continued to stay in the barn for almost six months, and their survival story was filled with moments of fear, tension, and uncertainty. When the war was over they made their way towards the border.

When the gentleman finished his story, I felt that all of us in the room were connected to him. The whole crowd stood up in a show of respect. Some people cried. I could not believe that someone younger than me had to go through something like this to save his own life.

The different moods and tones in the speaker's voice made the biggest impression on me. I was so focussed on the story and his presentation that I felt that I was actually with him and his sister, going through what they had gone through. I felt the fear, sadness, and suspense. This was an experience that I will not forget.

This story changed my thinking about the Holocaust. For me it is no longer just an event in history or simply historical fact. The Holocaust now brings out emotions.

Jonathan Aronowitz, Gr.8
Leo Baeck (South) Day School, Toronto, Ontario

The Whole Story

"Talk to you in a few days, Anna."

As I hang up the phone, my two grown children, Alisa and Jason, ask to hear my story. "Tell the whole story, Mom." I take a deep breath and begin:

"When I was seven, I had a best friend named Anna. One day she came to my house with her family and they stayed for many days."

I pause to remember what she looked like then.

"At first, she came downstairs to eat with us and play games with us, but after a while she stopped. Then her family moved into the attic, which I thought was a strange place to live. I asked my father why they were up there, but he said, 'It doesn't matter. Just don't tell anyone.'

"That night, I was in my room, almost asleep, when I heard loud shouting outside our house and banging on our door."

I look at my children, wondering if I should continue with the story or leave it at that. I decide to keep going.

"I quickly slipped down the stairs to be with my parents. I was terrified. My mother clutched my hand and whispered, 'I love you.'

"At that moment, the door flew open. A tall man with an impressive uniform and a quick stride entered our house, pushed my parents aside, and his soldiers began searching. They dragged Anna's family out the door.

"Before they returned, my mother quietly opened a small desk drawer, pressed something into my hand and told me to hide in the attic. I ran upstairs and squeezed into an old trunk. Sharp points of metal stabbed at my skin. It was very uncomfortable, but something told me not to move. I heard loud bangs, crashes, and gunshots. I was too afraid to make any noise.

Thinking of what is coming next in my story makes me want to stop again. Then I look at my children, their patient eyes staring into mine. I want them to know how brave my parents were, so I keep going.

"Hours later, I cautiously climbed out of the trunk and crept down the stairs. The first thing I saw were my lifeless parents lying on the floor. It was a terrible, shocking sight."

Suddenly I'm there again, the memory as clear as day.

"I fell to the ground and cried for hours. Then there was a knock on the slightly opened door. With a scream on my lips, I saw my uncle cautiously appear in the doorway. I raced to the door and sobbed in his open arms. At that moment I realized that the item my mother had put in my hand was still there. It was a note."

I reach into my pocket, take out a worn piece of paper, and read it to my children.

"Regina, we love you so much! I hope one day you understand what is happening in this war. Don't let anyone stop you from being friends with a Jew. And if you must die for your beliefs, die with your head high. Don't lose hope! I know you will make it through this and know you will make us proud!

Love, Mama and Papa"

I stare at the note for a moment, remembering the first time I read it. I look at Alisa; she is crying, and Jason is frowning. Alisa asks, "Anna? Is that the friend you were just talking to on the phone?"

"Yes," I reply with a smile. "The night my parents were killed, she and her family were taken by the Nazis to a concentration camp, and she was one of the few survivors. My parents were shot for hiding her family. I am very proud of my parents for helping to keep her safe and for standing up for what was right."

Alisa and Jason look at each other, and then Jason says, "People should hear her story, too."

I ask myself why I didn't cry when I told the story. Perhaps I feel a sense of pride from my parents' actions and understand their purpose.

Alisa exclaims, "Mom, you should write a story so others will understand the importance of the legacy they left behind."

Brittany Caron, Gr.7
Bonaventure Meadows Public School, London, Ontario

Generous and Brave

Io ho letto un libro intitolato "Un posto sicuro". Il libro parlava di Edith, una bambina che era stata nascosta in un collegio francese da alcune persone che avevano dedicato la loro vita a salvare gli ebrei.

Secondo me queste persone sono state molto brave e generose e meritano la nostra stima perché hanno rischiato la loro vita per salvarne molte altre. Se io fossi stato una di queste persone che vennero salvate mi sarei sentito molto felice perché, come in una fiaba, sarebbe stato un esempio di come il bene alla fine vince sempre.

Anche se per vincere il male si devono superare molte difficoltà bisogna sempre avere la speranza.

I read a book called *Hiding Edith*.[xi] The book was about a little girl who was hidden in a French boarding school by some people who had dedicated their lives to saving Jews. I think these people were very generous and brave, and deserve our respect because they risked their lives to save many others. If I was one of those people who was saved I would feel very happy because, just like in a fairy tale, this would be an example of good always winning in the end. Although in conquering evil one must overcome many difficulties, we must always have hope.

Francesco Martinez
Istituto Comprensivo Thiesi, Sardinia, Italy

Irena Sendler: An Inspiration

To honor an amazing person in history, I chose to write an imagined interview with Irena Sendler based on her fascinating life. Irena Sendler saved thousands of children from the Warsaw Ghetto during the Holocaust.

Q. *So Irena, could you tell me a little about your background?*
A. Before the war I was a Polish Catholic social worker and humanitarian. I served in the Polish Underground and the Zegota resistance in German-occupied Warsaw during World War II. My father died in February 1917 of typhus. Many of his patients were Jewish. I was greatly influenced by my father, who died when I was seven. His last words to me were, "If you see someone drowning, you must jump in and try to save them, even if you do not know how to swim." After my father died, Jewish community leaders offered to pay for my education. I was suspended from Warsaw University for three years because I opposed the ghetto-bench

system, which segregated Jews in university, forcing them to sit apart from others. In 1939 the Germans invaded Poland. During 1942 and '43 I found adoptive families for all the rescued Jewish children. It was hard to convince parents to give up their children. Parents would ask, "Can you guarantee that they will live?" But all that I could guarantee was that they would die if they stayed. It was even harder to convince the Polish adoptive parents to take the Jewish children. My code name was 'Jolanta'. In 2007, I was nominated for the Nobel Peace Prize.

Q. *When were you born?*
A. I was born on February 15, 1910 in Otwock, Poland.

Q. *What are your religious beliefs?*
A. I am a Roman Catholic.

Q. *How did you travel back and forth through the Ghetto with children, without getting caught?*
A. With help from two other Zegota members, I was able to save 2,500 Jewish children. We smuggled them out of the Warsaw Ghetto providing them with false documents and sheltering them in individual and group children's homes outside of the Ghetto. Some children were smuggled out in gunnysacks or body bags. Others were buried among loads of goods. One baby was smuggled out by a mechanic inside of his tool box. Some escaped by entering a church with one door opening to the Ghetto and the other door to the Aryan side of Warsaw. They entered as Jews but left as 'Christians.'

Q. *Were you afraid of the consequences of going in and out of the Ghetto saving innocent children's lives?*
A. At first I was afraid of getting caught, but it also felt good to be able to save so many lives.

Q. *Why did you risk your life to save a bunch of strangers?*
A. Because I was not going to let thousands of innocent children die just because they were Jewish.

Q. *Are there any other parts of your story that you would like to share with me today?*
A. On October 20, 1943, I was arrested, imprisoned, and tortured by the Gestapo. My feet and legs were broken, and I was sentenced to death. I ended up in the Pawiak prison, but no one could break my spirit. Zegota saved me from my death by bribing the German soldiers on the way to my execution.

Irena Sendler died on May 12, 2008. She was 98 years old. Irena's story was almost forgotten until 1999, when a group of four students from Union Town High School, in Kansas, researched her story and wrote a play entitled *Life in a Jar*. Later, in 2009, that play was adapted into a made-for-TV movie, entitled *The Courageous Heart of Irena Sendler*,[xii] which was my introduction to her amazing story. She did not take credit for her actions. She was quoted as saying, "I could have done more. This regret will follow me to my death." She also said, "Every child saved with my help is the justification of my existence on this earth, and not a title to glory."[xiii]

It is so easy for stories of true heroes to get lost over time. I hope Irena's story inspires you as much as it has inspired me.

Devon K. Donkervoort, Gr.7
Princess Anne French Immersion Public School, London, Ontario

A Single Wish
Dedicated to Trudy Kokx

At night, I am curled up in my bed with Beertje. Her soft puppy body lies beside mine, rising and falling as she snores gently. The faint sound of the enemy planes overhead becomes a nightmarish lullaby. Every night, I stay up late listening to the roaring engines and watching the flickering plane lights. The nauseating smell of petrol reaches me and I cover my nostrils with my scratchy, gray blanket. There is just one question going through the head of everyone involved in this war. When will these times end? It could be tomorrow, or in a week, maybe a month, likely a year! I don't understand why the Nazis don't like Jews. My best friend, Silke, is a Jew. She is funny, pretty, and extremely friendly. Silke is also very hard-working, as are her parents. Do Adolf Hitler and the Nazis have something against hard workers?

Since the Nazis took over, everything has become – what is that word *Moeder*[10] uses – scarce? Moeder cannot make my favorite cookies,

---

[10] Dutch for mother

anymore. She says the ration tickets do not allow it. *Vader*[11] cannot smoke his big cigar anymore, but I am okay with that. I just do not understand why everyone is punished because Hitler is controlling everything! When I ask Moeder my many questions, she sighs and answers, "Henrietta, you and Gertrude are very mature for girls of ten, but I am not prepared to answer your questions." No one gives us answers anymore.

There are thirteen children in my family – nine girls and four boys. I am the seventh girl in the family and my twin sister, Gerti (Gertrude) is three minutes younger than me. We live in Sloterdijk, a small town near Den Haag. There is a river running through our town and many large boats to watch. Regretfully, Moeder wants us to stay closer to home, so we may no longer go to watch the boats.

We have real raid drills quite often at school. I have come to hate bells and sirens. There are sirens for air raids, sirens for village raids, bells for lunch, and bells for school. The bells and sirens in my day cut it up into thin slices. I love to play dress-up with Gerti and Silke. My favorite costume is my maid outfit. I wear it over to Silke's all the time. We use old, empty apple crates as our chairs. Sometimes, we pretend that there is an air raid in a big castle and Princess Silke has to hide.

One day, Silke, Gerti, and I were playing the princess and maids as usual at Silke's house while her parents were away. Suddenly, another wailing siren sounded, followed by silence. At first no one in the village made a sound, but suddenly we heard the neighbor's door open and shut quickly.

---

[11] Dutch for father

"Raid! The Nazis are here!" our neighbor cried. Silke stood there frozen in fear. I grabbed her hand and yanked her under one of the crates we were playing with. I shoved Gerti under another one and sat on top of the empty one. My heart pounded in my chest so hard that I thought it would leap out of my body.

Two German soldiers in muddy boots walked into Silke's house. As I sat, shaking on top of the empty box, one of the German soldiers came up to me and spoke to me in broken Dutch. He shoved me roughly off the crate and lifted it up. He threw it back on the floor and shook his head at his companion. "The boxes are empty," he snapped in German, without checking the other ones. He spat on the floor and stomped away to check the rest of the house. The two soldiers came back through the kitchen minutes later and left the house angrily,

I heard a soft knock from the inside of Silke's box and I kicked it gently to tell her it was safe to come out. At first, the crate lifted slowly, and then she jumped out and leaped into my arms. "You are my best friend!" she whispered in my ear and then she put on her princess voice and said, "How may I ever repay you?"

I looked at her for a moment, and I answered her in my maid voice. "There need not be a payment for my foolishness and fear, dear princess."

Gerti smiled at me as she slowly extracted herself from the box. "You are a true hero, dearest sister."

Olivia Hivon, Gr.7
École secondaire catholique Père-René-de-Galinée, Cambridge, Ontario

Hidden in the Attic

The Journal of John Hoekstra

June 8, 1944

My name is John Hoekstra. I live in Nazi-occupied Holland. My wife died before the war. I have five children who each have their own children. I live alone in my house; the upstairs has been closed off for years to save the cost of heating it. There are currently three Jewish families hiding up there. No one except me knows this, not even my grandson, Allen, who visits me every day. Since it has been closed for so long, no one is suspicious. If the Nazis discovered these families, they would kill them along with my family, and me. These Jews have been living here since the second year of the war without any problem. They know that they have to be silent and discreet so they will not be discovered. I am writing this at great risk. My journal cannot be found or all will be lost.

June 10, 1944

After months of what seems like a walk through a dark, dreary tunnel, a light is starting to shine at the end. The Allies have started to make their way through Normandy and France. What a wonderful sign that Hitler's reign may soon be over! But for now, I am still petrified that the Nazis will come and take away the Jews hiding upstairs, and me along with them. I envy those who do not live in this terrifying time, for they do not have to fear the wrath of Hitler.

July 2, 1944

The Allies may be in Europe, but that has not discouraged the Nazi troops here from being so wretched. Our neighbor, Toonis Roobhgiern, has been holding back some of his milk to be able to feed his family, and the soldiers found out. They came and took him to the front yard, called his family and all the neighbors to watch him get shot. The looks on the children's faces were just appalling. I did not think people could be so heartless. I do not know what his poor wife and children will do. I fear for my son's life because he has been skimming the grain to feed his family. I do not think I will be able to sleep tonight.

July 23, 1944

The Allies have penetrated deeper into Europe! There is a rumor that they are on their way here to the Netherlands. Today I was taking some extra food upstairs to the families and one of the children came up to me and said, "Sir, you are my hero."

I replied, "I am just doing what I feel is right." This made me feel like everything I have done is worth it. Am I a hero?

August 19, 1944

My worst fear has come true; the Nazis came to search my house. I heard a knock on the door. I went to open it, thinking it was my grandson. But instead, a flood of fear and doom washed over me as I tried to act as though I was not guilty of anything. My heart was pounding as the soldiers said, "We are here to search your house." I prayed that this journal was hidden well enough so it would not be found and that this would not be the one time something went wrong upstairs. The soldiers headed to the bookshelves where I kept my journal. They started to pull out every book and flip through it. Then one soldier picked up the journal. My breathing became very heavy, my heart was racing, and it felt as if it was pounding in my ears. Just as I was ready to knock the book out of his hand there was a noise upstairs.

Braedon Hoekstra, Gr.8
Monsignor Morrison Catholic School, St. Thomas, Ontario

Cayley McAllister, Gr.8
Eugene Reimer Middle School, Abbotsford, British Columbia

Chapter 6

Not Everyone Is Willing to Help

The sad truth is that there were too many people who supported the Nazis and what they were doing during the Holocaust. One of the biggest mistakes we can make is to think that the Holocaust happened because of just one person – Adolf Hitler. Yes, it's true that he was a monster and proclaimed a set of beliefs that were hostile and bigoted. But the massacre of millions of people happens only when there are many others on board. Hitler did not work alone. He had military and political leaders in Germany and other countries who supported him fully. And in almost every country that was occupied, the Nazis found ordinary citizens who were willing to cooperate with them and help in the persecution of Jews. That's a hard truth to face but it's one that must be stated.

Certainly, there are many people who followed the directives of the Nazis simply because they did not want to get involved in the problems of others, namely the Jews. Many felt that it was easier at that time to keep their heads down and ignore what was happening to their Jewish neighbors. Many non-Jewish individuals worried about their own safety and what would happen to their families if they reached out to help. That fear was genuine; we know that the punishment for helping Jews was harsh. But there were also many who actually believed that Jews and others were inferior and should be eliminated from society. And those people eagerly turned on the Jews in their communities and literally handed them over to the Nazis. Some even took the Nazis up on their offers to pay for Jews who were turned over to them.

As important as it is to celebrate those individuals who helped Jews during the war, it's equally important to know that many did not. Here are the stories of some people who cooperated with the Nazis. It's only by facing these stories that we stand a chance of defeating injustice in the future.

How Can I Be Proud?

September 7, 1939

I am a man who has been called many things: a bomber pilot, a Nazi, a friend, and even a murderer. But never would I refer to myself as proud. How could I be as I watch innocent people shiver and shake in the bitter cold? Skin and bones. Pride does not exist in me. I am part of the establishment that has left the Jews to die. Children, whose faces are etched with fear, haunt me as howls of pain echo through the air. How has humanity allowed this to happen? My heart is a barren wasteland, home to evil secrets. It no longer holds love but only anguish and regret. My mind desperately tries to hold on to happiness, the golden times. But now, every time I look out the window, the further away happiness appears and the closer sadness gets. The images swirl around in my head, poking and prodding at what remains of my resolve. Tears roll down my cheeks.

Obediently, I carry out the command and release the bombs on the innocent. The orange flames engulf the crumpled buildings leaving nothing but scorched remains. I cringe, shut my eyes as tight as I can, and plug my ears to silence the pain that rages deep inside me. To the Jews the world is war and they are the forgotten seedlings sown into the black earth of death. I am one of the many farmers who has sown and harvested the Jews. And yet, the Jews regard me as proud as I march by with my head held high and my gun slung over my shoulder. Some of the battered ones, their heads high too, follow me at a distance, unarmed, down the dingy street saying painful words that sting. And so I ask, "How can I be proud?"

Emma Sandri, Gr.6
Pope John Paul II Elementary School, Bolton, Ontario

Going Back

Dear Sarah,

It was July 23, 1944, though I didn't know it at the time. I, of course, had lost track of the day and month. This was the day when the Soviet army came and freed all of the prisoners from Majdanek. I couldn't keep in all of my emotions anymore, so I cried. I cried tears of joy because our son, David, had survived. But I cried tears of pain because you, my Sarah, my beautiful wife, had not.

We prisoners rushed the gates, all fearing that they might shut, or all of this would end up being a dream. When I got out, I tried to find David. It took me what seemed like forever, but I found him where water was being given out. He was smiling. I think the last time I saw him smile was before we were transferred here.

"Papa, where are we going to go now?"

"To our house, I think."

It took us two weeks, but we finally got to Rzeszòw. As David and I walked along the streets we could see the people staring and whispering. Whether they were words of spite and hate, or words of guilt or pity, I didn't know. Either way, we were still outcasts, and no one held out a hand to us. We approached our house and, to our disappointment, the lights were on.

I walked up to the door and knocked on it softly at first, but nobody answered. I was about to knock again when a woman answered the door. She looked me up and down and then looked at David. A panicked expression crossed her face.

"Alfons," she cried, "can you come here now?"

"What is it?" said the husband as he came to the door. His wife whispered something into his ear.

"Why are you here?"

"Well, you see," I began. "This was my house before my family was taken away, and it's still my house."

"Listen," Alfons started, "this is our house now and you can't just take it from us."

"You honestly think that I want to come back and live here?" I asked him. Alfons looked surprised at this, but his wife spoke before he could.

"It *is* a lovely house."

I was starting to get angry now, and I rarely showed anger. I just couldn't believe how inhumanly blind these people were.

"I know that it's a lovely house!" I practically shouted. "My wife also thought that this was a beautiful house. But do you think that I can just come back and live in a community that obviously doesn't want me and my son? Do you think that I want to live around people that gave my family up to the Nazis so easily? How am I supposed to trust my old friends or send my son to school? So you can take this house and our spot in the community, because we don't want either of them!"

"What does your wife think of this choice?" the wife asked. I then switched from anger to silence.

"Oh, I'm so sorry," she said.

No you're not, I thought to myself. *If you were sorry you wouldn't have acted as if we were criminals when we came to your doorway.*

"Let's just go, Papa," David said.

But before we could leave, the woman said, "Please come inside. Don't you want to see what happened to your house?"

So here I am now, my Sarah, walking through rooms of memories. They kept the dining room color the same. I wanted the walls to be yellow, but you were always the one with better taste. You chose a baby blue. I remember that day so well; you were five months pregnant with David. How am I supposed to choose colors now for a new house without you? I'm now walking into what was our sitting room. The couple who live here fixed the crack in the wall. I remember that you always hated that crack. Whenever David would draw a picture, you would try to hide the crack with it. Oh Sarah, I'm looking at our back garden now. The flowers are in bloom! This was our dream house, Sarah. But it's time to let go of it. I promise that I will start a new life for our family. I will get David and myself to America so that we can make our lives great again. I love you and miss you so much, Sarah, and I wish you were here.

Emma Friedman, Gr.8
Robbins Hebrew Academy, Toronto, Ontario

We Are Not Born to Hate

One Holocaust survivor, Eva Olsson, feels that children are not born with hate. They are not born racist, sexist, or prejudiced. Hate is something they learn. These words inspired me to write about this, because I know that hate still exists today in many forms.

Kindergarten children do not care whether their friends have blond hair or blue eyes, or have a different skin color, or where they go to worship. Children in the Holocaust could not see or understand why a war was needed. Young German boys and girls were brainwashed with lies against other people, and young Jewish children were discriminated against.

German children were not born with a desire to threaten, or to want power over the Jewish race. They did not form opinions about these important issues on their own. They heard ideas and words from family members and authority figures in their community.

Most children see their parents as role models. They want to be like them and talk like them. Many German children realized as adults that the racist thoughts they grew up with only reflected what their parents believed about the Nazi regime.

My *Opa*[12] was a young German boy who was only four years old when the war started in 1939. Originally his family was very 'pro Hitler' because Hitler had helped the country in the years following the First World War. But they changed their minds after *Kristallnacht*, the "Night of Broken Glass." His family did not agree with the senseless harming of

[12] German for grandfather

Jews who were their countrymen. After the war, however, my Opa, still a young boy, was very afraid of the American soldiers because they had bombed his city. German newspapers reported that the Americans were there to kill them all. When the Americans came to his house, he hid in the basement, terrified, only to find that when they did come downstairs, they were very nice to him. In fact, they gave him his very first Hershey's chocolate bar. Then he understood that he had believed the lies the Nazis had told him, and that the Americans had only come to help.

Hate in our world has impacted greatly on the human population. We should all know that we have to stop racism and hatred. Small acts of kindness can help start to make the world a better place. If only we could preserve the innocence that every child is born with, then we as human beings could learn to accept our differences and strive for a hate-free world.

Anna Prust, Gr.8
Forest Hill Public School, Midhurst, Ontario

War Changes Lives

Imagine living in a place where you can trust none of your neighbors, where you must savor every last scrap of food your family gets. Not having the freedom to do what you want or go where you wish. Being forced to leave your family. During World War II, in most of Europe, families lived like this. The German soldiers overran the countries of Europe, including Belgium. As they took over Belgium, they changed the lives of many.

At the beginning of the war, my great-grandfather remembered the sky being black with German bombers. It was May 10, 1940, his birthday. German planes would crash regularly in nearby fields, becoming part of the new landscape.

When the Germans first arrived, all Belgians had to relinquish their cameras and guns to the Germans. Motorcycles were used to reinforce the Belgian army. Either way, personal possessions became part of the war.

Even with the war around them, Belgians had to continue their everyday lives. My grandmother's parents married in 1941. They had three children by the end of the war. My grandmother was born in the basement, in order to be protected from the dangers outside. My grandfather's parents got married in 1940, and by the end of the war they had four children, including my grandfather.

My great-grandparents were all farmers. Farmers were expected to provide the Germans with a portion of their crops, milk, butter, and potatoes. So, Belgian farmers hid food from the Germans. My grandfather's dad hid their milk and butter in the stream near their house, to keep it cold. My grandmother's dad hid their food in the basement wall. When he built their house in 1942, he included a secret compartment.

The war taught many how to save. Crops were harvested, stored, hidden, and used throughout the year. Milk, eggs, meat, and all of the animal parts were eaten. Nothing was thrown away. People walked along the railroad tracks collecting chunks of coal that had fallen off the trains to heat their houses.

People were much more desperate in cities since they relied on buying their food. City relatives, whom farmers hadn't seen in years, would come, starving, wanting food for their families. They would normally never visit, but they were desperate. Therefore, a city family sent one of their sons to work on my great-grandfather's farm for free, if they provided him with food. Finally, as the Germans retreated at the end of the war, young German soldiers needed transportation to get home. They wanted my great-grandfather's horse, harness, and cart. He tried explaining to the Germans that the horse was still wild. This was interpreted as a refusal to hand over the horse, so the Germans held a gun to my great-grandfather's head. He quickly said that they could take what they wanted. My great-grandfather retrieved his horse and cart in the next town only days later. The Germans left the horse and cart there when they realized the horse was wild.

After the war, every town dealt with its "stool pigeons". They were the people who collaborated with the Germans and were rewarded by them. At the end of the war, the townspeople would find the stool pigeons, shave their heads, and shun them.

Living in the midst of a war changes people. War brings out the worst in people – stealing, betraying, pillaging, killing – and it can also bring out the best in people – sharing, helping, caring, and working together. No one should have to live through this. These memories will haunt Belgians forever. Here in Canada, we are fortunate enough not to have this kind of past. But imagine living this way. It must take really strong character to survive.

Melanie Piché, Gr.8
Princess Anne French Immersion Public School, London, Ontario

Taking a Stand

Fear is what caused many people to ignore what was happening during the Holocaust, and to refuse to help their neighbors.

We need to do what is right even if we are scared. As Martin Luther King Jr. said, "Cowardice asks the question – is it safe? Expediency asks the question – is it politic? Vanity asks the question – is it popular? But conscience asks the question – is it right? And there comes a time when one must take a position that is neither safe, nor politic, nor popular; but one must take it because it is right."[xiv] Sadly, there are still wars being fought because of religion, race, culture, or beliefs. In North America, Europeans began to destroy the culture of the Aboriginal peoples. More recent examples would be the Serbian/Croatian conflict that took place between 1991 and 1995 because of disputes over land. As well, approximately 800,000 Tutsis were killed in the 1994 Rwandan genocide.[xv]

We need to teach people to empathize with others. If you can understand how another person feels and put yourself in his or her shoes, then changes can happen. People who helped the Jews in World War II had this ability. They were able to ask themselves, "What if this was happening to me and my family?" We need to remember that even though we may have many differences, we are all human beings who deserve respect, empathy, and love.

We can prevent history from repeating itself by never forgetting our past. I think in honor of those who suffered and lost their lives in the Holocaust, on January 27, International Holocaust Remembrance Day, we should wear yellow to symbolize the yellow Star of David that the Jewish people were forced to wear by the Nazis.

Jocelyn Toupin, Gr.7
Minesing Central School, Minesing, Ontario

Parry Brar, Gr.8
Eugene Reimer Middle School, Abbotsford, British Columbia

The Bruise

Dear Diary,

Today, just like every day, I walked with my brother to school; it was a cold day in September. Isaac was shuffling his feet while kicking all the leaves away to make a path. I was walking behind him counting the cracks in the sidewalk. I knew that I had one hundred and fifty-two more to count before we finally turned the corner to our school.

My classroom was full of students' colorful artwork and writing. I loved being able to express my feelings through drawings and paintings. My favorite was the painting I made of my home. I remember spending all of my allowance on the paints and canvas. I recall how much time it took me to blend the perfect combination of colors. That picture truly represented the sense of safety I felt at home. My parents loved it; they always knew how to make me feel proud of myself.

After a long day at school, I was eager to go home. I ran home with Isaac and rushed through the front door. I found my mother sitting at the table, peeling carrots for soup. I smelled the delicious aroma of chicken broth. Mama signalled for Isaac and me to sit beside her so we could tell her about our day. The time that the three of us spent together was always very special.

On this afternoon, Isaac was quiet and withdrawn, unlike his typical seven-year-old self, who was often jumpy and loud. He had large bruises on his arm that I hadn't noticed, since I was in such a rush to tell my mother about my day. Mama and I sat looking awkwardly at each other; no one said a word. Her eyes unlocked from mine and slowly made their way down to Isaac's arm. Her face looked shocked; her forehead became tense and worried. She asked him about his day and he just dismissed it and shook his head. Mama repeated the question in a more concerned voice. He quietly mumbled that he had been in a fight at school with a few boys who were yelling that Jews were disgusting. He tried to get them to stop, but they wouldn't. Isaac said that they challenged him to make them stop as they held him down and punched him in the arm. Isaac didn't know what they had against Jews, or what the red, black, and white spider patch on their sleeves meant, and neither did I. Isaac kept repeating that he didn't understand why being Jewish was so bad.

After he finished, Mama embraced us. We were told to go to our rooms and wash for dinner. I followed Isaac up the stairs to my room and hurried back down as soon as I was ready to eat. All I could think about was being the first to give Papa a hug when he came home from work. When I was halfway down the stairs, I was surprised to see Papa and Mama sitting at the table with worried faces. I overheard Mama repeat the story that Isaac had told her about school. Papa tried to reassure my mother that everything was going to be okay, but it looked like Papa was the one who needed to be reassured. From the looks on their faces, I knew something was terribly wrong. I was so scared to go to school the next day. Should I be ashamed of being Jewish? Should I hide my religious identity for safety? Do you think I'll be next?

I need your help, Diary.

Sierra Palaci, Gr.8
Leo Baeck Day School (North Campus), Toronto, Ontario

Chapter 7

How Will We Ever Survive?

Fear was one of the primary emotions that Jews and other victims faced during the Holocaust, and it was indeed overwhelming. But despair was, perhaps, even more unbearable.

Jewish families had to endure the pain of seeing loved ones taken away from them as they were deported to concentration camps. They witnessed their mothers, fathers, grandmothers dying or being killed in front of their eyes. They endured constant cruelty from Nazi soldiers. And through it all, they must have asked themselves: When will the suffering end? How much more can I take? Drained of their physical strength, their emotional strength also began to deteriorate, plunging them into hopelessness.

"...people today have the means to live, but no meaning to live for."[13] These are the words of Viktor Frankl, a respected psychiatrist who

---

[13] Frankl, Viktor. *Man's Search for Meaning*, New York: Washington Square Press, 1959. Print.

was born in Vienna, Austria in 1905. In 1942, along with his wife and parents, Frankl was deported to the Terezin concentration camp where he worked first as a physician and then as a psychiatrist. He tried to turn the despair he saw all around him into something meaningful. That was his approach to working with patients who had arrived in Terezin and were overcome with shock and grief – to find meaning in the suffering. Frankl was the only member of his family to survive the concentration camp. After the war, he continued to practise as a psychiatrist. He wrote many books about the psychological effects of life in a concentration camp. There are institutes and forms of therapy named after Frankl to this day.

Despair was a real part of the suffering that many Jews had to endure. Try to understand this devastating feeling as you read the stories that follow.

Annika Ah-Chow, Gr.8
Gordon B. Attersley Public School, Oshawa, Ontario

The Interview

The interview at twelve o'clock kept coming to my mind. All I could think about was breaking down in the middle of it, on camera. When I got there, the cameras started rolling, and the words started pouring out.

"In 1940, I was taken from my house in Poznan, Poland, onto a train. My parents wouldn't explain anything, but they probably knew just as little as I did. At the age of fifteen, I was so lost. All I could think about was my little brother, Jacob. He was eight at the time and probably scared out of his mind. In neighborhood after neighborhood, every Jewish family had been taken away.

"As we were loaded onto the vehicle, I smelled a horrible smell. I could barely breathe in this dark, cold train. There was no food for us, and we had no idea what was going on.

"Three days we were on that train, and during that time all I did was think. I didn't talk, not even when my parents asked me something. But my mind was exploding with questions. What was happening? Where were we going? Would I survive?

"Eventually, the train began to slow down. My stomach felt so empty, yet I didn't even want to think about food. The train stopped, and as the door opened, I stood up. I needed to get out of there.

"We stood behind barbed wire and were ordered to split up. Some women and children would go to the left, but my whole family was sent to the right. Then I was separated from my father and brother. My father kissed me on the cheek and told me to listen to the soldiers. I know that he wanted to comfort me. I walked to the left. Little did I realize that would be the last time I saw my father and brother.

"My mother and I walked in a single file. No one could begin to fathom where we were. After a few minutes, we stopped and stepped into a large building. We were told to strip off our clothes and change into the new ones that were given to us. Every one of the uniforms had a number on it. Mine was 98288. They told me that this was to be my identity. They said I was a *dirty Jew*, not even worthy of having a name.

"I was in this camp for five months. Every day people were taken away, never to return. I can remember my mother telling me not to worry, but this didn't help. It felt as if I were trapped in a glass bottle and couldn't get out. Days went on, then weeks. I thought of my father and brother and wondered what life would have been like if I wasn't locked away in this godforsaken camp.

"One day, the soldiers told us to get into two groups: women and children. I went into the women's group, of course. They told my mother to step out of the group along with several other women. All of them had to stand in a line and be silent. As I stood there watching, they shot the women one by one. That was the last time I saw *any* of my family.

"A few weeks later, American soldiers came to my camp and rescued us. They helped me emigrate to America, all alone with the clothes on my back."

Now, I am sitting in front of this camera telling you my story. I don't know why God chose me to stay alive. Sometimes, to be honest, I wish I wasn't.

Elizabeth Segal, Gr.8
B'nai Shalom Day School, Greensboro, North Carolina

Difficult to Forget

Le persecuzioni contro gli ebrei sono iniziate con cattiverie senza motivo. Mi dispiace per tutto quello che è capitato con l'Olocausto, per tutti quelli che non hanno avuto un futuro e soprattutto per i bambini che non capivano quello che stava loro accadendo.

Immagino che sia stato difficile per chi è sopravissuto dimenticare tutto quello che era successo: affrontare il campo di concentramento, vivere in mezzo alla sporcizia, alle malattie e alla fame. Deve essere stato difficile dimenticare i brutti pensieri.

The persecution against Jews began with hatred for no reason. I'm sorry about everything that happened in the Holocaust, about those who did not have a future, and especially about children who did not understand what was happening to them.

It must be difficult for those who survived to forget everything that happened, having faced the concentration camps, the filth, the disease, and the hunger that they lived with. It must be difficult to forget the ugly thoughts.

Francielle Dore
Istituto Comprensivo Thiesi, Sardinia, Italy

Fight for Survival

The sound of children wailing and the cry in a mother's voice. The roar of the train's wheels crashing against the metal railway tracks. This was all Ettie could hear as she rode that filthy train to the death camps. She was alone in that moment, her parents lost in the crowd of crying people. Her head, full of long matted brown hair, turned to see a father all alone with his young son lying limp in his arms. She saw the fear and sadness in this father's eyes, the eyes that would never see his son's smile again.

That memory never left Ettie's mind. It never left when she was shoved off that disgusting train. And it was still there as she was stripped, showered, and shaved.

Many months later, Ettie was still in that death camp. And the image of that father and son haunted her dreams as she slept, not so soundly, on the hard pallet. Her body was jammed up against three others, and the stench was almost unbearable. This night, Ettie's dreaming was cut short as screams and the blast of gunshots crashed through her sleep. *What is going on?* Ettie thought, as bedmates started to move around restlessly. An elbow to Ettie's fragile rib cage caused her to let out a loud yelp.

"RAUS AUS DEM BETT!" Get out of bed! The loud call of Nazi officers rang through Ettie's ears. She quickly did as she was told, her skeleton-like limbs flying out of bed and onto the cold ground. But the Jewish prisoners weren't lined up as usual, and it seemed too early for roll call. Ettie, along with many of the other girls, turned their heads in confusion. She began to hear low whispers that were being passed from mouth to mouth.

"What's going on?"

"Are they taking us away?"

"I'm scared!"

Ettie kept her mouth shut as she was shoved back and forth. More gunshots went off, but she guessed they were only to strike fear in the girls' hearts so they would stop talking. Confused, they were all pushed out of their building and into the freezing night. Ettie shivered from both fear and the cold. "March!" A tall Nazi officer held his gun high in the air as he bellowed out orders. Cold white snow fell gently upon their pale faces as Ettie and the other girls started to march out of the camp.

Why are we leaving? Ettie's eyes scanned her surroundings. *Are we being let go? Is the war finally over?* A small shot of excitement ran through her. But she soon found out that this march was not a march to their freedom, but a march to their death.

Three days now, three days without rest, with little food, and no water. Ettie's already empty stomach cried for food. Her fragile body craved rest, but there never was any. Ettie's hopes of ever being free were quickly fading. People were dying all around her. If you were not able to keep up, or if you looked weak, the officers would simply shoot you. There were bodies lying everywhere as Ettie marched with frozen, bleeding feet to her unknown destination.

Ettie's body was very weak, but she refused to give up. Every time she felt like dropping to the ground, she would remind herself of that father and son from the train. The son had no chance at all; he died on the long trip. And the father had probably died quickly, giving up because of a broken heart. She had seen many give up, just wanting to die rather than face such a life. But Ettie's will was strong. She had lasted this long and knew she could last longer. She would not lose this battle against the cold, the hunger, and the pain. She would fight for survival.

Samantha Olivia Robbins Wall, Gr.8
Bonaventure Meadows Public School, London, Ontario

Remembering Sonya

From my bedroom window, I could see soldiers marching up and down the street. It was strange to see that they were so close to our house. I wondered what they were doing. Someone stumbled outside of my bedroom door. It was my mother. Ever since my father moved away, she had been very angry with me and my brothers.

"Heidi, what are you doing looking out of that window again? You are not allowed."

"But Mama…"

"We are going to board up that window tonight. Do you understand?"

"Yes," I mumbled.

The next morning I was startled by screeching that sounded like desperate screams coming from outside. I slowly pulled the covers from my bed and quietly walked over to my bedroom window. It was boarded up. Though Mama had indeed kept her promise of keeping me from the events outside, I needed to see what was going on. I needed to see who was in trouble and who needed help. While I was trying to pull the boards off, I realized there was a hole at the top of the window. I grabbed a stool, stepped onto it, and saw my friend, Sonya, and her family being dragged away by soldiers and put into the back of a truck. *Why were they pushing her family around? Why were the soldiers doing this to them? I thought soldiers were supposed to protect and help people.*

My heart was pounding as I flew down the stairs. I was thinking so much about Sonya that I lost my balance and fell down the last ten steps, landing on my knees. My hands felt numb, my feet felt cold, and it felt like someone had thrown a rock at my head.

"Wake up Heidi. Wake up!" yelled my brother Edward. It was hard to open my eyes. My eyelids felt as heavy as bricks.

"Why am I in the hospital?" I asked.

"You fell down the stairs at home and you had a concussion. Why were you running down the stairs so fast?" he asked me.

"I saw the soldiers taking Sonya and her family and dragging them out of their home against their will. Why were they doing that to them, Edward?"

"Mama doesn't really want me to tell you this, but I think you should know. The rumors are terrible." I felt my heart stop as I listened to Edward tell me where he heard Jewish families like Sonya's were being taken. I shivered, and goose bumps covered my body knowing that my friend might be someplace horrible. I could barely sleep that night; just thinking about her made me almost cry and wonder what was happening in our world.

The next day was a blur to me. School carried on, but it was difficult to focus. The memory of Sonya's family sobbing played over and over in my head. I wished she was still here sitting next to me, making me laugh.

Many years later, I found myself at the gates of Auschwitz concentration camp. This is where my best friend, Sonya, and her family died like so many others. These were our soldiers – German soldiers that took her young life. I could picture Sonya, once happy in the playground of our school, but images of her, helpless behind these terrible gates, became too clear. She has never left my thoughts.

Ava Berry, Gr.6
The Study School, Toronto, Ontario

The Beginning of the End

Tuesday, August 17th 1938,

I have always wondered what causes rain. It is calming to some people, but to me it is just noisy. I hate it. Mother told me yesterday that God controls rain, telling it to fall. She says He controls everything. If this were true, why would He make Father die? Why would He make everyone think Jews were pigs; that we do not deserve to walk on the earth because of our religion? No, I believe that Mother is wrong. God doesn't control everything. Not even rain.

Wednesday, August 18th, 1938,

One of my neighbors jumped off a roof today as I watched from my window. The woman screamed at God in the clouds and then, still screaming, she threw herself over the edge. She lay in a lump on the street, not moving. Soon it seemed that the whole neighborhood and others passing by were on the street and watching as the woman's family carried her from the street and into the house. After, another family appeared with their bags and belongings and announced they were leaving and anyone was welcome to join them. The family had decided things were getting too dangerous living here, and they thought that any day the Nazis would ship them off somewhere. Many families decided to leave. I have no idea what God is doing letting these people take us away. I have no idea what He is thinking.

Thursday December 19th 1938,

The trucks came. They took the first Jews, and the rest of us have gone into hiding. My mother keeps complaining because I should not be writing and should be praying. I do not know if praying will solve anything since so many horrible events have happened, and God hasn't helped us in any way. Mother says we should be proud to be Jews and not hide. For once I agree! Still, my family and I are all hiding in a hidden closet in the basement and believe me, we are packed in like sardines in a can. There are three of us in here: my mother, my sister and I. Shayna keeps on crying that there are rats and that they will eat her toes. Mother is doing her best to keep her quiet. I have very little light to see what I am writing and very little room. I am crouched on the floor in a ball, writing as fast as I can because my heart is racing. I feel that any second the door will swing open and my family and I will be separated from each other – forever! I will put up a fight. They cannot hurt me. No, I am strong. I will escape to America with my family and live a life – a real one, not one hiding my face because of my religion.

Footsteps above my head. My hand is shaking and I cannot breathe. I am strong, and proud to be a Jew. The door swings open.

Annie Peterson, Gr.7
Glenview Senior Public School, Toronto, Ontario

So Many Children

I found a photo of children peering over a barbed wire fence in a concentration camp. It was so compelling. The children's faces looked cheerless and bewildered.

One thing you should know is that more than 1.2 million children died in the concentration camps.[xvii] Older children were more likely to survive in the camps because they could be assigned to forced labor. The children's chances of survival varied greatly depending on how well they could work. Many young Jewish women were simply forced to be prostitutes.

In the photo, some of the children look to be about five years old. They look innocent, though their expressions are anguished. It is very depressing to think that people were treated so badly whether they were young or old, male or female. They did nothing to deserve this horrible treatment, and that thought makes me want to weep. These children hardly had a chance to live their lives. I will pray for all the survivors and their families. I know that this was a devastating time in human history. I want to learn more and hope to someday go to the United States Holocaust Memorial Museum in Washington D.C.

Jillian McGarry, Gr.6
Hamburg Middle School, Hamburg, New York

Indifference

I was jolted awake by the sound of bombs again this morning. Mother is reassuring, but Father's blank stare troubles me. The reverberation of bombs pounding the earth's surface is well known to me. The Nazi occupation of our neighborhood is a certainty. Is tonight the night my family will hear the knock at our door that will change our lives forever?

The streets are almost deserted now. The Jews who dare to walk in daylight are easily recognizable. Beyond the Star of David sewn to their clothing is the unspeakable fear in their eyes and the wretched expression on their faces. Father once said, "Indifference will seal our fate, my beloved, not the Nazis." Father has lost all hope. We live in constant fear of the soldiers. Mother is becoming pale. Tonight, I'll fall asleep to her soft, muffled weeping. Is hope slipping away from her, too? I must be strong and courageous for my family. I must help them see beyond the dark cloud of humiliation and indifference that stains the light of the world. We will endure. God promised to never abandon His people. Aren't we still His people?

Analia Silveira, Gr.6
Pope John Paul II Elementary School, Bolton, Ontario

All That I Have

Caro diario,

Ogni giorno passano le camionette dei nazisti che prendono qua e là gli ebrei per portarli nei campi di concentramento, dove danno poco da mangiare e si dorme al freddo. Io penso che non sia giusto morire e finire in un forno crematorio. Mi voglio nascondere permettermi al sicuro. Penso che però prima o poi mi scopriranno e morir. Tu sei tutto quello che ho. Tu parlerai per me diario.

Dear Diary,

Every day trucks pass with Nazis driving here and there, rounding up Jews to bring them to concentration camps where they are given little to eat and where they sleep in the cold. I do not think it right to die and end up in a crematorium. I want to hide to keep myself safe. But I think sooner or later I will be discovered and I will die. You are all that I have. You will talk for me, Diary.

Marco Meloni
Istituto Comprensivo Thiesi, Sardinia, Italy

In the Shadow of the Oak

I look around me and see faces. Some faces I do not know and some are family, but we look the same, with that same mask of terror and confusion. We are all cramped in an attic, hoping that we are not next and that our loved ones will be okay. Thank God for Miss Schroeder for shielding us from the lingering black smoke on the horizon.

Today is Friday, and this day has dragged on laboriously. Miss Schroeder wanted us to be comfortable, so we moved almost all of the furniture upstairs. The room is still slightly damp and dusty – so much so, that I can barely stop sneezing. Even though she lives in a big house, dinner is always scarce as Miss Schroeder is not a wealthy woman. Everyone appreciates the fact that we have chairs and couches to sit and lay on.

I look at my watch; it is 1:30 a.m. How I want to go outside to smell the air and forget for just a minute that I am hiding. Before I can talk myself out of it, I am walking down the stairs swiftly and quietly. The stairs squeak and groan, as if they want to keep me there. The brisk night air hits me like a cold snowball. I inhale the warm and familiar scent of chimney smoke. Sooner than I can even think about it, I am walking down familiar streets. I look back at the house that has become my prison. It is red brick with big white windows and curtains that are always closed.

I soon find myself in the main part of town, not more than two miles from my hiding place. At first I don't hear them, but then the voices grow louder. I turn the corner, shielded by a great oak. A family is being loaded into a truck. Soldiers are carrying them away. The stars pinned on their jackets mark their destiny. The little boy struggles to be with his father. The soldiers grab him and push him to the floor while kicking him.

I gasp and gaze up at the great oak that looks so old and proud. This oak has been here for hundreds of years, protecting the people it towers over. In that moment, I make up my mind and a blood-curdling scream erupts from my mouth. The soldier's eyes turn. He lets go of the boy who runs to his father. From here everything is a bit hazy, and it hurts my body and soul to think about what actually happened under the oak's protruding branches.

I find myself, the next day, on a cattle train with many others. I hope Miss Schroeder will arrive before the train departs, but sadly this doesn't happen. The train halts abruptly, the doors open, and all I can see is a huge brick wall with soldiers surrounding it. I look towards the black smoke rising.

Emma Kilbourne, Gr.8
The Study School, Toronto, Ontario

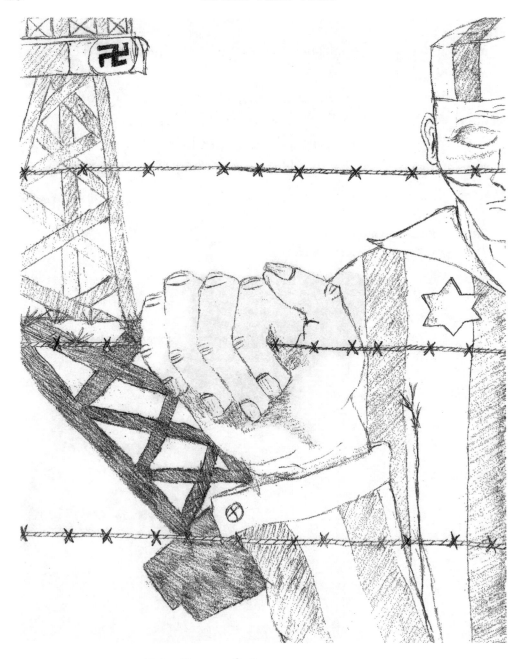

Dylan Rogers, Gr.8
Eugene Reimer Middle School, Abbotsford, British Columbia

Chapter 8

It Comes Down to Luck

When I speak to young people about the Holocaust, I often ask them what they think it took for someone to survive. The answers I get are varied and interesting. Some young people think that strength was the key to survival. Others think that faith may have been most important. Still others tell me that staying healthy would have made the difference between life and death. All of those answers have some truth to them. It certainly helped to be strong and healthy. Faith gave people hope, and that too was helpful. Other factors such as youth, having money, having someone to live for, being strong, etc. were also important. But if you ask a survivor what it took to stay alive, the answer that you will hear most frequently is that it all boiled down to luck.

The truth is that some Jews who survived were rich and some were poor. There were survivors who were short and survivors who were tall; some who were educated and others who had little or no schooling; those who were strong and those who were weak; some who were observant and others who had cast their faith aside. Old, young, male, female, determined or indecisive – all of these attributes were there among those who survived and among those who did not. Luck was the common denominator for all of the survivors.

One of the "luckiest" survivors whom I have ever met was Bob Kornhauser. Bob managed to either escape from or elude arrest by the Nazis an astounding eleven times! He certainly had great cunning and ingenuity. But he was the first to admit that he was also very lucky. He, like many others, managed to make it to the end of the war, though it is also important to know that many of his family members perished. They were not as lucky as he was.

The stories that you are about to read tell of some remarkable instances of luck – being in the right place at the right moment when others were clearly not as fortunate.

It Could Have Been Me

Being a Jew in Nazi-invaded countries in Europe meant that you lived in constant fear. Soldiers could burst into your home any time. They could grab you on the street at any moment, send you to a labor camp, a concentration camp, or worse, they could kill you on the spot. At the labor camps you would be forced to work from the early hours of the morning to late hours of the evening, barely given any food or any time to sleep. In the concentration camps, you would suffer humiliation, ridicule, starvation, and disease. You were unlikely to survive.

If I were a thirteen-year-old Jewish girl living in Europe at the time of the Second World War, I would be forced to wear a yellow star, and I would no longer be allowed to go many places. I would be turned away from certain stores. I would be prevented from going to school. I would have my bicycle taken away, my personal and prized possessions, my books, but most of all, my freedom.

My family would have to move to a small room inside the Nazi-created ghetto in our town because we would no longer be welcome in our neighborhood. We would go from having three full meals a day to barely having enough for one, due to the food shortages and rations. Since the ghettos were filled with Jewish people, almost every day many were sent to concentration camps. The Nazis would continue to force Jews onto trains and trucks until the entire ghetto was empty. And yet in no time at all, the abandoned ghetto apartments would be filled with new Jewish families sent to live there. This was the circle of Jewish life during World War II, and only the lucky survived.

If I were one of those to be sent away from the ghetto, I would probably go to a concentration camp. If we were sent to a death camp, we would be divided into two lines: those who were deemed strong enough to work, and those who were not. Many women and children were in the second line. Since I am tall, I may have passed for a woman and been sent with those who would live, but because of my age I may have been put with the children and sent to die.

Upon arrival, many would go to the showers. These weren't normal showers, though. You never knew if you would be getting water or poisonous gas, if this would be your last breath, or if you would live another day.

As I think about how I could have been treated during the Second World War, I am shocked and appalled at the inhumane things that the Nazis got away with. Recently, my family found out that we are of Jewish heritage on my grandmother's side of the family. They lived in the Ukraine before they fled to Canada. I grew up believing that they had moved here because they wanted freedom from the government that was in control during the late 1920s. But now we think that it was because they were Jewish; even before World War II, terrible things were happening to Jewish people in Europe. If my great-grandparents hadn't come to Canada, these events could have actually happened to people in my family – perhaps to me.

Julie Hernden, Gr.8
Kedron Public School, Oshawa, Ontario

My Papa

My grandfather's name is Walter Absil, and he is one of the most inspirational figures in my life. Walter was born in Vienna, Austria in 1924, fifteen years before the Holocaust. His story is very different. He survived because he was lucky. He was also smart. This is why he is my inspiration.

When the Nazis rounded up his family, Papa and his sister were not home. When they returned, a neighbor explained to them what had happened and told them to leave. At the age of sixteen, Papa and his sister, Lisel, found themselves all alone in the middle of a war. Papa did his best to protect Lisel, but soon realized she was too young, and if they were both going to survive, he needed to find her a safe place to live. He brought her to a nearby convent where the nuns took her in. Just imagine what was going through my grandfather's mind; he had just lost his parents and was about to give up his younger sister. At sixteen, he was all alone.

Papa then left the city and went to the countryside where it was safer. He got a job working on a farm because most of the workers were gone, forced to join the army. Life on the farm was not easy. He worked very hard and was not treated well. He slept in the barn and in the winter it was very cold. He was not even paid for the work he did. But my grandfather was smart. He often took what little money he had and bought tobacco from the Belgian soldiers and sold it to Polish prisoners. He then used that money to buy food and anything he needed to survive.

I am in awe of Papa's story. I could not imagine having to do what he did in order to survive. I cannot imagine having to care for my brother in the way that my grandfather cared for his sister. At any time, Papa could have given up. He could have told himself, "The Nazis are looking for me. I am going to die anyway, so why even try?" My grandfather couldn't save his parents, but he did save two lives – his own and Lisel's, and from those two lives came four generations of people. Because he was not in the concentration camps, Papa is one of many undocumented survivors of the Holocaust. His story is not only unique, but inspirational. Whenever I am having a rough day, I think of Papa and what he had to go through. Because of him I am here today, sharing his story with you.

Charlie Ornstein, Gr.6
Jewish People's and Peretz School (JPPS), Montreal, Quebec

All by Myself

December 16, 1940

Dear Diary,

It is me, Michael. Being a thirteen-year-old boy during these troubled times is hard. Living in the Warsaw ghetto has been terrifying.

Before this, I lived at home with my parents. One day, they said they were going out to town, but they never came back. I was scared, nervous, and alone. The German soldiers have been separating families, and here I am, all by myself.

I have a feeling my parents might have been taken to a concentration camp. My only thought is to find them, and escape to freedom. Many have tried to run away, and have failed. Some children have escaped through the wall at night. The risk is great, but I have nothing to lose. My desire for freedom is strong, and I want nothing more than to see my parents again.

December 17, 1940

There are rumors that freedom is just across the border in Czechoslovakia. I have scraps of food and warm clothes for the long, cold journey ahead. I hope to run at night, and sleep during the day so the soldiers don't find me. I traded my father's old wristwatch for a compass to help me find my way. My best friend, Stanislaus, has given me the address of his cousin, Bertha, who gives Jewish people shelter and food. I hope she will also provide me with clues as to where to find my parents.

I hope the necklace with the Star of David that my mother once gave me will bring me luck on my dangerous journey ahead.

December 18, 1940

I've had a stroke of luck. It snowed heavily, but that helped me escape without a problem. I hid on the back of a wagon that was leaving town. In a few hours we reached a deep forest, and that's where I got off. I followed my compass south and found a barn to hide in. It had hay and animals to keep me warm, and some old apples to eat.

It took one long, cold day and night traveling through the forest to reach the border. I knew soldiers were near, so I hid in a wagon. The wagon was searched, but I curled up inside a small box. It was very uncomfortable, but worth it. After many hours, the wagon stopped in a small town. I didn't know I was free until I heard a strange language.

I was afraid, but a nice farmer helped me. I told him about Stanislaus' cousin Bertha, and he knew her last name. She lived in a small town called Zelno. He gave me bread and a ride to Bertha's. By nightfall we arrived at a dimly lit cottage. Bertha's family was very kind. They gave me warm food and a place to sleep.

Freedom is wonderful, and Bertha's family has pledged to help me find my parents. I am very hopeful that they are alive, but thank God I'm alive too.

Sean Bermingham, Gr.6
Hamburg Middle School, Hamburg, New York

Captured by the Gestapo

I'm scared. No, I'm terrified. I know what's happening. I see it with my own two eyes, but I still cannot believe it is true. The Gestapo found all of us — me, my three sisters, and even David, my little nephew. I heard the most terrifying rumors about the concentration camps. They torture you. It is so unbearable, all this waiting as they decide where and who to put you with. Little David is scared and his mother is anxious. So I say that I will watch him. All is going fine until the Gestapo officer finally tells us where to go. David and I are put on a truck. David can't bear to be without his mother any longer, so he shouts, just as the truck is about to leave, "MAMA!"

The officer asks me, "He's not your kid?" and I shake my head, no. Then he tells me to get off the truck, and tells David's mother to get on.

Later, I overhear two other prisoners saying, "Good thing you aren't on that truck. It's taking the people to their deaths." I know I must live. I know that if I escape I can tell people what happened. That's what my sister and David would have wanted. One day gone, two lives gone, and a close call for myself. BUT I WILL ESCAPE.

This story was based on a true story told to me by my grandmother, who was talking about her mother. My great-grandmother did escape in the end, with a bullet wound, lived a happy life, and died of old age.

Sam Estreicer, Gr.7
Glenview Senior Public School, Toronto, Ontario

Trapped

What was that?

You stop breathing for a moment, straining every inch of your body to hear. Anything – a sound, a whisper.

You hear the dull thud of heavy footsteps. You feel the hairs on your neck stand up. A door creaks open.

Surely, no one knows where you are hiding. A cold sweat begins. You feel as though the world is spinning.

The footsteps grow louder, coming nearer to the door you hide behind – the bookcase, the hiding place that's been your safe haven for so long.

You look to your family, your own fear illuminated in their eyes. The footsteps stop, and you are caught. You brace yourself for what you know is coming – the pain, maybe death. You freeze as you hear a pounding on the wall. No one moves; silent tears flood your eyes and drip down your cheeks. Your mouth forms into a silent scream.

But then something happens.

You hear, "All clear." And two sets of boots leave the room, carrying their owners far away, marching back to receive their next orders. You wonder how those men can be so eager to hurt, to please their master.

As the boots march away, stamping a death cry, you are thankful that those boots didn't reach you.

Your mouth forms a smile.

Teri Simone, Gr.7
Wheatley School, St. Catharines, Ontario

Chapter 9

We Have to Have Hope

It is remarkable to me that there were so many people who managed to remain hopeful during the horrors of the Holocaust. I can't imagine how it would be possible to have everything taken away, be imprisoned, lose loved ones, and still hold on to hope – to still have some dreams and wishes left.

Those who were struggling to stay alive during this time probably had two kinds of hopes. The smaller ones – more like wishes – would have been for food, a warm coat in freezing temperatures, shoes that didn't have holes in them, warm water in which to bathe, or to be free of lice and other things that plagued Jews on a daily basis. Ruth Uszerowicz Malc was only sixteen when she was sent, first to the Dachau concentration camp, and then to Auschwitz. She was the only one of her family of eleven to survive. Years later, Ruth was asked what things she dreamed about during her imprisonment in the concentration camps. Her answer was, "I dreamed about a piece of bread and butter." These were the everyday hopes.

The bigger hopes had to do with survival. Many survivors will say that they hoped that the end of the war would come swiftly and that they would be alive to see it. Most Jews hoped that they would be reunited with loved ones who had been taken from them. It's certainly likely that Jewish parents hoped that their children would survive even if they themselves did not. Some hoped that they would live to see the day when their oppressors would be punished for what they had done.

Raoul Wallenberg was a Swedish businessman and diplomat who is best known for his efforts to rescue tens of thousands of Jews in Nazi-occupied Hungary in the latter days of the Second World War. Because of his position as a special envoy to Sweden, he was able to issue protective passports to Jews who were destined for deportation to the concentration camps, thus saving their lives. On January 17, 1945, Wallenberg was arrested by Soviet authorities. He was reported to have died in prison in 1947, though the circumstances of his death remain a mystery to this day. During his courageous lifetime, he provided hope to thousands who were targeted by Nazi hatred.

Having hope gave Jews and other victims a purpose – something to keep them going when they were in their darkest moments. Read the stories of other Jews who vowed that they would never lose hope.

Ilana Ivry, Gr.8
Thornhill Public School, Thornhill, Ontario

The Journal

November 5, 1939

Today is my birthday! Because my family does not have much money, I've received very few presents, except for this journal. It's not much, but I am happy with it. It's a wonderful deep red, thick journal, with a long, glossy ribbon in it for a bookmark. The bookmark is exactly the same shade as the leather. Paired with it is a pen and inkpot. I didn't know what to write about at first, but Papa told me to write about myself. "Let the journal get to know you." So I will.

My name is Joseph Aaronson. I am the only son of Adam and Chava Aaronson. I like to write, especially haikus, even though they are very uncommon in Germany. I have learned that they are three line poems where the first line has five syllables, the second has seven, and the third has five again.

I am Jewish, and thirteen years old.

I am not able to have a Bar Mitzvah because all the Jews in Germany have been forced into hiding or they might be arrested. It isn't safe to go out in the streets anymore, let alone have a Bar Mitzvah. Nazis prowl the streets, searching for "dirty, scabby Jews" to kill. As a result, my family is hiding in the cellar of Mr. Strept, a former colleague of my father. Before my papa lost his job, he and Mr. Strept were in the same bakery business. It's not too bad; we are safe, fed, and hidden. To pass the time, I can write in this journal, like this haiku:

An empty canvas,
This journal will soon be filled
With my life's story.

I showed what I wrote to Mama, and she smiled and ruffled my hair. "Good, Joseph. Write every day, and you'll become a writer!" I think I would like that.

November 12, 1939

Mama and Papa are growing very upset. They say we must move, and soon. "But why, Mama? We are already safe in Mr. Strept's basement. With the hidden door, no one will see us!" I said.

"But they can hear us, Joseph," Papa answered me. "Your mama has been pregnant eight months already, and when she does give birth, this tiny cellar will not hold four of us!" His words are true. Mama is obviously pregnant, her belly distending noticeably. Every day, Papa and I put our ear against her, hoping for even the smallest signs of a kick. If the baby started to cry out, loud enough for any Nazis to hear, who knows what would happen?

So far, none of the letters to relatives have been answered, not even the ones we sent to Uncle Max in America. But Mama and Papa and I keep waiting.

To wait for freedom
Makes children quite impatient,
And adults, anxious

November 19, 1939

The Nazis nearly found us today. We were eating breakfast when Mr. Strept pushed through the trap door in a panic. "Hide! The Nazis are coming! Go behind the boxes, furniture, anything!"

"Wha–?" my question was cut off by Papa's hand.

He scolded me as I was dragged behind a mouldy couch. "Don't talk, boy! Are you trying to get us caught?"

By the time I quieted down, the shouting started. "Come out, you damn Jews! We know you're in there! Get out, now!" Pounding sounds rained down in the silence, and at last there was a *thud,* the sign that the front door had been broken down. All of us waited, but no Germans burst through the trapdoor. No rifles were pointed at us. We all realized at the same time that it was our neighbors we heard being searched. We were safe, but not untouched. Mama even broke down and started to cry. "This has been too close! Adam, we must get away! Now!" she wailed.

"Chava, no place in Germany is safe anymore! I promise you, we will leave this country as soon as possible, but you must stay strong until then!"

None of us will get to sleep easily tonight.
Nazis prowl the streets
Searching for the Jews, their prey.
Will we soon be next?

December 20, 1942

So much time has passed, and now there is nowhere to run. I was nearly asleep when a sudden stop jolted me alert. The train was no longer moving and the doors were shifting, widening until they were fully open. Light streamed in almost too quickly to adjust to, and many of us covered our eyes. A few of us near the doors were brave enough to look out to see where we were.

"This place smells like death!" Exclamations pierced the air. A girl my age fainted, but did not fall. There was no room for that. Guards approached, toting rifles pointed at us.

"Everyone is to exit the train immediately! Do not take your belongings with you! They are to stay on the train!" they barked coarsely. I was forced off the train, leaving my precious journal behind me. I no longer have it with me and fear I will never see it again.

We were approached by yet more uniformed men who bombarded us with questions. Some people were sent to the left, others to the right. Somehow, my mother managed to push through the others milling about and whispered to me, "When the guards ask you your age, tell them you are sixteen. It will not be hard to believe, given your size. Survive, Joseph."

Soon after, a Nazi grabbed her by the shoulder along with my baby brother. They were immediately sent to the left, with many of the others.

"You there, boy, how old are you?" he asked me next.

I stuttered, "S-sixteen, s-s-sir." The man in front of me scanned me from head to toe with his eyes, and I could almost see the scepticism in them. But finally, seeing how tall I was, he seemed satisfied. With a nod and a shove, I was sent to the right where others were lined up.

"All of you are to take off your clothes, now!" we were ordered. "Strip naked!" We had no choice but to obey, and now we did not even own the clothes on our backs. "From now on, you will not have a name, and will only be addressed by a number tattooed on your arm!" I became 40268. "Now line up!"

Only when I was in my barrack did I have time to think about what had happened to my family. Where could they be? I was all alone.

Tomorrow we begin working. I am lying on a plank of wood in our cold barrack with hundreds of other people. Though my journal was taken away, I'm going to keep my promise to Mama and keep writing in it, if only in my own head. I'll do whatever it takes to remain sane and live! For Mama and Papa. It's hard to sleep. The noises and smells of the many people here suffocate me.

I'm scared.

Countless victims here
Suffer for their religion
Yet we've done nothing

February 1, 1946

Uncle Max opened the door. "Ah! You're here! Come in, come in!"

I stepped hesitantly, clean for the first time in years, well dressed, and safe. On January 27, I was freed by the Soviet army from the hell named Auschwitz. After taking my name, officers found the same Uncle Max my parents had written to before we were captured. He had gotten visas for us after all, but by the time they had come for us, they were too late. I am safe in America now.

"Sit down. I have something for you." I did as he asked, and Uncle Max placed something in front of me. Crisp white pages were bound by blood-red leather. A glossy red ribbon trailed from the top of the book to the bottom, shiny and smooth. It was a journal, an identical twin to the one I had received on my birthday. An empty page stared at me, begging to be filled with words. "Your mama told me in her letters how you liked to write. She would have liked you to have this." He handed me a pen.

Hands trembling and unsteady, I began to write.
Determination
Will push us to be much more
Than who we are now.

Melinda Zhou, Gr.8
MacGregor Public School, Waterloo, Ontario

Slammed Shut

The heavy wooden doors slammed shut, and the little boy could tell that the strange men in uniforms had barred it from the outside. The telltale click of a lock chased away anyone's hope of escaping.

The boy blinked in the dark. He could not see anything past the bodies of other children, all standing up; there was no room for sitting. Soon, he gave up trying to figure out where he was; his thoughts were elsewhere, but too jumbled for him to make sense of anything. Earlier, he and his family had been sitting down enjoying breakfast. Now his porridge was left, half-eaten and knocked over on the dining room table. The same men in uniforms had rounded them up and herded them into lines here at the train station.

He remembered that his parents had told him the strange men in uniforms were the Nazi soldiers. He did not know what that meant. He did not know who the Nazis were or what they did, and he didn't care – until they took his parents away. The little boy had tried to cling to his mother, but was knocked aside roughly into the crowd of other crying children. He himself had started crying then, sobbing out of pain, confusion, and frustration. Just what right did they have to take his parents away from him?

Despite his protests, the boy was forced to watch his parents being led away into a large cattle car. He did not know what that meant. Were they going to the same place as he was? Would they meet up again when they arrived there? He could hear the other children screaming and weeping and oddly enough, he felt the need to stay strong for his parents, the other children, and himself. He wiped his tear-stained face.

The car they had been loaded into definitely seemed smaller than the ones he had seen the adults go into. The boy wondered if the car that his parents were in was better. Could they lie down? Did they all have enough space, or were they crammed together like he was? Immediately, tears started welling up in his eyes again. Just the thought of his family made him sad. His parents never did tell him where his grandparents had gone; one day they just suddenly stopped visiting.

"Where are we going?" a young voice asked. The little boy craned his head, and could just make out the silhouette of a girl about his height. Nobody answered her.

Time passed. How long had it been since they had breathed fresh air? How far had they travelled? Suddenly, an overpowering stench washed over the whole cattle car. Many of the younger children gagged and spluttered, and the older ones breathed in through their mouths. The boy did a little of both. The heat of midsummer, mingled with the sweat and stench, had some children retching. The little boy couldn't see. It was too dark, but he definitely heard a few thumps – the sounds of bodies falling against the wooden floor. The boy felt nauseous himself.

His vision seemed blurry, and he felt too squeezed by those around him to breathe properly. He was also thirsty, but no one came with food or water, especially not the Nazi soldiers.

Suddenly, a beam of light shot down from the ceiling of the cattle car. The little boy strained his neck and looked up. There was a tiny window, but it was too high up for anyone to reach. Sunlight streamed in through the opening, and the boy's eyes were blinded for a moment. It must have been around noon for the sun to shine so brightly. Despite the heat of the sunlight, his surroundings, and his growling stomach, the boy felt hope. As long as there was a sun in the sky with people living under it, someone would definitely come to help them. The little boy thought of his own family and the families of others he didn't even know.

Even if he himself didn't understand what was happening to him, he had to keep believing that someone else out there definitely would.

Amelia Zhang, Gr.8
Fieldstone Day School, Toronto, Ontario

I Still Have Hope

Dear Diary,

I don't understand why the guards are doing this to us. Why are they treating Jewish people like we are nothing? My mother keeps telling me to stay strong and do what they say, but I'm exhausted. I don't want to do this anymore! They took my home, my family, and all of my possessions. It's just my mother and me now, defending ourselves.

I wish I could go back in time and try to change things. I wish I was still at home where I felt love from everyone who lived with me. I wish I still had all my friends and family. But now I'm stuck in a barrack with hundreds of other Jews trying to survive.

Every day my mother and I pray that we will soon get out of this place. But I can't help being scared all the time. I see people being dragged outside, and then suddenly there are gunshots! What if I'm next? What if they take my mother? I've already lost everyone else. If I lost her, there would be nothing else to live for.

Even worse is the fact that I haven't eaten for two days now. Since the guards only give us one bowl of soup each day, I have been sneaking my portion into my mother's bowl. She has been getting weaker and weaker so I need her to get better.

She always wonders why I'm done eating so quickly, but I tell her I was starving. Every time I ask my mother when we will return home, she ignores me. It's as if she has lost all hope. But I haven't! I'm going to make sure to always have hope no matter what, because that's what my father taught me. I miss him so much and still remember the last time I saw him.

We were sitting at home and all of a sudden soldiers burst through the door and arrested my father. As he was being dragged out of the house, he looked back at our family and his lips mouthed the words, "I love you." That was the last I saw of him. A few days later, my brother never returned home from school. My mother and I found out he had been beaten to death.

Now it's just me and my mother, and I don't know what else to do but sit here and wait to see what happens. I have lost everyone in my family except my mother, who has no hope. So it's up to me to believe that my mother and I will get out of here soon, and live the rest of our lives freely!

Taylor Oppersma, Gr.8
Grandview Public School, Oshawa, Ontario

If Only

Dear Anne Frank,

If you had the chance to come back to our world, I would tell you not to, because although life has changed, some people are still hated. Jews, blacks, homosexuals, and other types of "different" people are still discriminated against. People say that they will never let the Holocaust happen again, yet it has. There have been other genocides since then. Still, I promise you that someday, in the far future, this will all end.

A few years after the war ended, the Jews were given their own country, Israel. I went there a few years ago, and it is the most beautiful place I have ever seen. I'm sure that you would have loved going there. One of Israel's largest trading partners is Germany, which is surprising to me. You would have been so proud of Israel, that the government was able to forgive Germany and move forward.

If I could only ask you one question it would be, "Do you still think people are really good at heart?" Is it possible that you can think that the people who took away part of your childhood, made you hide and suffer, and killed you and millions of people are still good? You would probably say that they made a mistake, and everyone does, but how can you forgive someone for a mistake as big as this? There are terrorists, criminals, and other evil people in the world, and it is strange to think that they could all be good and have good intentions. I know that you would give me a very intelligent and wise answer, and I wish that there was some way that I could hear it.

Your story taught me so much. You taught me to always be optimistic. You stayed hopeful through your experience in the Annex, even though you were terrified of what could happen. You also taught me to be thankful for what I have. You were always happy with what you were given, even if it wasn't that much. I have everything I could ever want and need, and sometimes don't realize how lucky I am.

In the end, some of your dreams came true. In a strange way, your dream of becoming a movie star came true. A few years ago, a movie was made about you and your life in the Annex. Also, you have become a very famous author. Your father published your diary after the war, and it has changed many people's lives. If only you could be here to see and experience all of this.

You were such an amazing person who affected the world so much in such a short lifetime. I can only wonder how you would have changed the world if you were still here. I wish that I didn't have to wonder. I wish that I knew.

Amanda Werger, Gr.8
Robbins Hebrew Academy, Toronto, Ontario

The Hattner Memoirs

Charlotte Hattner removed her delicate violin from its case, placed it on her shoulder, and picked up the bow. She struck the first chord; the melody filled her soul, and out poured the inspiring music.

At supper that evening, Charlotte's father, Robert Hattner, complimented her on her beautiful violin piece. He told her that she was talented. She thanked her father and devoured the delicious supper.

"Emma. Charlotte. Tomorrow you two are going to visit Grandma. She is excited to see you!" said Charlotte's mother, Annie.

Charlotte and Emma spent the next day at their grandmother's house. Charlotte loved visiting her grandmother, who lived on her own. Grandma's mother had died, leaving her life a story unknown to Charlotte. Everyone said that it was devastating.

"How's my beautiful twelve-year-old?" asked her grandmother, walking into the kitchen. Charlotte greeted her grandmother with a warm hug.

Her grandmother walked over to the stove and turned it on. She asked Charlotte if she wanted to bake cookies. Charlotte nodded excitedly. That was one of her favorite things to do.

While they were eating the freshly baked cookies with Emma, Charlotte spoke up. "Grandma, I have a project that I have to do about my ancestors. Do you think that I could look up in the attic for ideas? You have so many treasures up there." Charlotte's grandmother nodded.

Charlotte carefully climbed the dusty ladder to the attic. She turned on the light and walked towards the far corner. The floorboards creaked as she knelt down. She blew the dust off an old trunk and carefully opened it. Inside was an old, dusty journal.

Charlotte opened the diary and on the first page it said, *I was saved by the music.* Charlotte held the brittle pages between her fingers and smelled the mustiness of the years past. She spent the next four hours engrossed in her great-grandmother's writing. She couldn't believe the horror that her great-grandmother had lived through, being forced to play lovely music for the nasty soldiers that held her captive in the concentration camp.

Charlotte climbed down the ladder, diary in hand and walked into the kitchen.

"Grandma! Look what I found!" called Charlotte excitedly.

Charlotte's grandmother glanced down at the old journal. She was speechless. Finally, she told Charlotte to sit down at the table beside her.

Grandma sighed and started to tell Charlotte more about those terrifying times.

After hearing the story of her great-grandmother's life, Charlotte didn't know what to say. She realized that this was a story everyone had been keeping from her. Now she understood why.

A few days later, Charlotte sat at her desk at school. She gripped her great-grandmother's diary in her right hand, and in her left, she held a scrapbook. The teacher called Charlotte's name. She stood up and walked to the front of the room.

"My presentation is about my great-grandmother, Elena Hattner. She was a musician who lived through the Holocaust. She played the piano." Charlotte paused.

"A few days ago, I found her diary. It has all of her thoughts and feelings about this horrible time. She was sent to a concentration camp when she was about my age, and she was all alone. The soldiers decided that they would keep her alive to play music and keep them entertained. All of her belongings were confiscated and if she spoke, the soldiers would not listen. She was there to serve them and that was all." Charlotte paused again.

"Musicians in the concentration camps gave each other hope. Hearing music lifted their spirits. Because my great-grandmother was a musician, she was not immediately killed. Performing for the guards was what kept her alive. I got my musical talent from her. When I was looking through the trunk, with the rest of her belongings, I found her favorite song."

Charlotte played her great-grandmother's favorite song on her violin. Everyone clapped.

She took out a picture of her great-grandmother when she was about Charlotte's age. As she held it up for the class, Charlotte realized that she looked just like her.

Charlotte's heart felt warm, as if her great-grandmother were standing next to her.

Alyssa Woods, Gr.7
École secondaire catholique Père-René-de-Galinée, Cambridge, Ontario

Survival:
My Family during the Holocaust Years

My name is Sierra Goldfinger. Three of my grandparents are Holocaust survivors: Netta Silverman, and Regina and Charles Goldfinger. They have shared their stories with many people, including me. My grandfather David Silverman was very fortunate and escaped the Holocaust because his family came to Canada after World War I. They know it's important to tell their stories, because we need to learn and understand what happened. I know that it is very important for me to pass on the stories of my grandparents to my peers so they can learn how the Holocaust affected the Jewish people then and now.

Netta Silverman was only a small child when she and her sisters were sent on the *Kindertransport* to London to escape the Holocaust. My grandmother was only eighteen months old and her two sisters were eight and six. To protect her valuables, my great-grandmother sewed her silver cutlery into the lining of their coats. They would have been killed if these belongings had been found. In London, the three sisters, Netta, Inga, and Evelyn were split up and taken to separate foster homes. Fortunately, my grandmother, Netta, was one of her foster parents' favorite children, and they always treated her with love and care. As soon as the war was over, my great-grandmother wanted to get her daughter, my grandmother, Netta, back. Unfortunately, Netta's foster parents didn't want to give her back to her biological mother. Her mother, Elsie, had to go to court and fight for custody of her child.

My grandfather Charlie lived in Poland, and was sent to a ghetto. From there, he was taken to Auschwitz. In Auschwitz most of his family was killed, but he survived because of his ability to be a "chameleon" and change jobs. When the Nazis needed him to be a bricklayer, he became one. When they needed a tailor, he became one. One of the commanders in Auschwitz even assigned him to be his personal tailor. "If you were useful, you would stay alive," my grandfather often said. Just like the sign over the gates of Auschwitz stated: "*Arbeit macht frei.*" (Work makes you free). My grandfather's work kept him alive. He still has his concentration camp number tattooed on his arm. His story and the tattooed number remind me of how strong he is.

Charlie's wife, Regina, has a very different survival story. She and a friend worked on a farm and said they were Polish girls looking for work. When things got worse for the Jews and it was no longer safe, the two young girls, aged fourteen, left and hid in a hole in the ground in the forest for a few years. Regina's decision to leave the farm enabled her to survive. Unfortunately, the rest of her family was killed. After three years, she was found and sent to Auschwitz. My grandmother Regina speaks about how at Auschwitz, the Nazis put shredded glass in the soup so that it would rip apart the insides of the Jewish prisoners who ate it. While there, she worked in the munitions factory putting guns together. What the Nazis did not know is that many of the workers, my grandmother included, tried to sabotage the workmanship by putting in the wrong parts. When the Holocaust was over, Regina held her head high and tried her best to start her life over again. Not long after the Jews were liberated, she met and married Charlie.

Learning about the Holocaust and about my family's history has taught me so much about how strong my family is. Despite everything that happened, they kept carrying on and did whatever they could to stay alive and safe. They never lost their faith or the hope that they would be rescued. They are true role models and people that I am proud to look up to and call my family. We must never forget our history and who we are. We are proud people with faith in God and we must make sure there is *tikkun olam*[14] in the world. We must all share in repairing the world so that it is a better place for our children and their children.

Sierra Goldfinger, Gr.8
Leo Baeck Day School (North Campus), Toronto, Ontario

Ernie Weiss

Be strong. After this cruelty, I promise you will leave this darkness and step into a new light. I see you sitting on the step alone in the corner. You're wearing trousers just above your black ankle boots; your white undershirt is hidden under your short sleeved shirt. You're tired, Papa, but I see the glint and promise in your eye that knows there is something meaningful ahead.

I also see the sadness in your soul that brings you back to the moments when you lost everyone. The stench of the trains, the sewage, the clanging of the tracks, crying, weeping, sadness – in one brief wave of a hand, it was all gone, lost forever.

How could you ever make sense of this? How could anyone? I can see your guilt, your shame, for you are the only one to survive from all seven. You don't know why yet, but I am here to tell you.

---

[14] A Hebrew expression that means to repair the world.

I am Edie, your third daughter, though you don't know me yet. I can't wait for you to meet Rachel, your soon-to-be-wife, and my mother. She's full of charisma and life. She knows nothing of the losses and that will be good for you. You would never want her to know your past because you don't want any pity. You now have a new life – that chance at the American dream. I know that now you have turned your back on God, a god that turned his back on you. But what lies ahead is enlightening and may be the only way that God can compensate you for what you have lost.

Now you stand at Ellis Island, coming into a foreign land – action, bustle, the lights of the big city, shoving, pushing, screaming – but this time not the darkness and the chaos of your past, but rather, the entrance to your future. Coca-Cola, vending machines, movie theaters, the privacy of your own room in a downtown hotel. This is payback, although you would never ever see it that way. These are the cards you were dealt; it's for you to figure out how to play the hand.

The way you were treated by the Jewish agencies upon your arrival in New York set the standard by which you decided to live your life – through *tzedakah*, the act of giving back. Instead of turning your horrific experience into bitterness, you turned it into gratitude, and from then on you made a choice about how to live your life. You have made a personal promise not to bury yourself in silence like many others, post-war. It is because of your courage and your strength that you speak out. This is how I have come to understand what life was like for you.

You still don't know why you are the one whom God chose to survive amongst your siblings, but you know that you owe two things to those who did not survive: the duty to remember and the responsibility to make your life count for something.

As you witnessed your father being taken away, little did you know then that in the future, my first son, Jonathan, would bear his name. They are very similar, you know – both smart and intuitive.

Now that you are gone, you will truly be missed by everyone who knew you. You were a kind, non-judgmental, beautiful man who made us feel important in your presence. You touched us with interest, respect, and warmth.

I watched you through your illness; you never complained or criticized. You thanked every one of your visitors for taking the time to see you. You were very grateful for every act of kindness that came your way. I will always remember the way you avoided questions about yourself, and turned the conversation in a different direction to show interest in others.

I would often ask you what you were thinking as you lay on the hospital bed. You wondered what would come next, and if you had been a good enough man. It's always the kindest people who never feel that they have done enough.

Ernie Weiss, my father, my greatest friend, you came out of the darkness with perseverance, bravery, and dedication to redirect your life, and make it the way you truly deserved. You are known as a hero by many. You will truly be missed.

Casey Stein, Gr.8
Leo Baeck Day School (South Campus), Toronto, Ontario

I Am a Little Canadian Girl

I am a little Canadian girl.

There is a war going on in a different country.

The year is 1942.

I don't like the way Hitler is treating the Jewish people!

It is not fair; we're all the same, but we have different religions.

I think we should all be friends and protect each other and live in peace.

I have a feeling I should do something, but I was told to stay out of it.

I hate that everyone is fighting.

I pray and pray at night, wishing all those little Jewish children will be safe just like me!

I wish they could all come here and live in freedom.

I have questions for you: Will this war ever end? Will we ever be friends?

I hope in our future all of us and I mean EVERYONE can live in harmony!

Dayna Antonucci, Gr.8
LaSalle Public School, LaSalle, Ontario

a solitary flame can light up darkness,
hope can be kindled even in despair,
we can wrest light from darkness
  — Navah Harlow

Antigone Fogel, Gr.7
Downtown Jewish Community School, Toronto, Ontario

Chapter 10

Looking for Justice

Before the Second World War began, there were roughly nine million Jews living in Europe. By the time the war ended in 1945, two thirds of those nine million – about six million Jews – had perished. In addition to the Jews, five million others also died or were killed, targeted by Hitler's campaign of hatred and discrimination. These five million included individuals who were physically or mentally handicapped, homosexuals, Roma, and others. That's a total of eleven million people who were killed. The Holocaust remains one of the worst genocides in history.

What about the perpetrators of this crime against humanity? What became of the Nazi commanders, political leaders, and others who plotted and worked together to carry out this massacre? In 1947, a series of military hearings took place in Germany, known as the Nuremberg Trials. The International Military Tribunal charged twenty-two prominent members of the Nazi leadership with war crimes. The accused included Hermann Goering, Rudolph Hess, Albert Speer, and others, people without whom the mass killings would not have been possible. Adolf Hitler, who would have been tried at these hearings, had committed suicide in the days leading up to the end of the war.

Many Jewish survivors were there to testify against these criminals, even though it must have been incredibly difficult for them to face the perpetrators and relive the horrors that they had suffered at their hands. Those who spoke showed great courage.

Of the twenty-two defendants at the Nuremberg Trials, twelve were given the death penalty, three were cleared, three were given life imprisonment and four were imprisoned for periods ranging from ten to twenty years. Since the end of the war, thousands of Nazi war criminals have been tried in countries like France, Poland, Canada, the U.S., and Germany. In many cases, it has been extremely difficult to locate these villains and bring them to justice. Many have managed to "disappear" by creating new identities in foreign countries. Governments have not always been willing to cooperate in returning these individuals to their home countries to stand trial. Nazi hunters like Simon Wiesenthal have tried to locate and track down those war criminals who managed to escape to other countries at the end of the war. His efforts have led to the capture of over one thousand Nazi criminals.

The stories that you will read here talk about justice and the importance of making amends for the horrors of what went on during the Holocaust. But while the Nuremberg Trials and the capture of others are important, the truth is that none of these arrests or imprisonments will ever make up for the lives that were lost or the pain and suffering that was endured by millions during the Holocaust.

Ledor Vador[15]

LUBLIN, POLAND – 1940

David, an outgoing ten-year old Jewish boy, is going to run into his little sister's room. There, he'll surprise and tickle Ruth while she giggles, as most three-year-olds do. He will find her blue stuffed rabbit, dubbed Shashi, to play peek-a-boo with Ruth. The room will be filled with laughter, joy, and – RING! – the timer in the kitchen will go off as David starts sprinting down the stairs. He will strain his famous *pierogi* and put them on a serving plate. Waltzing into the dining room, he'll set them down, proud of his creation. David has always wanted to be a professional chef, but knows that with the terrible anti-Semitism that affects every part of life, it will not be a possibility.

Everyone will gather to taste David's concoction. Ruth will smile and clap her hands, while his father will say, "Ah, Davidel, you have just outdone yourself! These are delicious." Everyone will enjoy, but his mother will just stare blankly out the window, as though looking for the pattern of the stars. "Don't you like my food?" David will ask. She will then bow her head. He will frown and say, "Mama, what's wrong?" Her eyes will close, and open with tears. "Something is going to happen." She'll pause. "And it will not be good."

BROOKLYN, NEW YORK – 1942

Sylvia, a blissfully happy ten-year-old girl, cradles her baby sister lovingly in her arms. The baby's laugh is innocent, as Ruth's always was. Once

---

[15] A Hebrew expression that means from generation to generation.

Sylvia sets her in her crib, the baby peacefully drifts off to sleep. Sylvia creeps down the stairs, careful not to wake her sister.

The soldier sits at his desk, engulfed in the scent of fresh bread from the kitchen and old leather books on the shelves. He studies and smoothes the fur of a stuffed, blue toy rabbit. He puts it to his face and takes a deep, painful breath. Sylvia dances into the room with a smile. She sees the anguish in his eyes. Puzzled, she asks her brother, "What's wrong, Leonard?" He lifts his head to look out the window at the budding spring flowers and whispers, "Something is happening, Syl. And it is not good."

AUSCHWITZ, POLAND – JANUARY 25, 1945
An American soldier shivers in the emptied camp, the bloodstained snow making him nauseous. He wanders the area solemnly. His eye catches something buried deep in the snow. He digs and pulls out a soaked, tattered blue toy rabbit with torn fabric, stuffing pouring out, and broken button eyes. The soldier holds the rabbit to his heart and cries.

PHILADELPHIA, PENNSYLVANIA – 1972
Sylvia laughs and slaps her knee while watching television and chomping on popcorn. "Come on, Sonia!" she yells to her daughter, "you're missing it!"

Sonia, her ten-year-old, enters the living room with a blue toy rabbit in her hand. "What's this, Mom?" she asks. "I found it while I was cleaning out my closet."

Sylvia puts her hand to her mouth. She takes the rabbit and hugs it to her chest. Sonia does not understand. "What's wrong?" Sylvia sighs and wipes her eyes. "Something happened, sweetie, and it wasn't good."

GREENSBORO, NORTH CAROLINA – PRESENT

Sonia sits on the bed with her ten-year-old daughter, Elise, as they talk and discuss the day. "You made the team? Oh, congratulations, Elli. That's great!" Sonia says. Her proud smile suddenly turns to the worried look of David's mother. She leaves the room without explanation. When she returns, she has a stuffed blue rabbit in her hands that she says is named Shashi. It is freshly sewn. This is not the Shashi that witnessed the suffering of her owner through button eyes, nor the Shashi that was ripped almost to nothing. It is not the Shashi that was dropped when Ruth was taken for a "shower," and not the one with tears soaked into her fabric. It is not the Shashi liberated from the Polish snow, nor the one that endured such indescribable sorrow. This is not the Shashi that brought sadness and memories of horror, but one that brings comfort and hope.

Sonia hands Shashi to Elise. Elise is confused. "What is this, Mom?" Sonia hesitates. "This is not going to be easy, sweetie, but you need to know." Her eyes begin to water as she continues. "Something happened long ago, and it wasn't good. But," she says with Shashi held to her heart, "may it *never* happen again."

Jordan Segal, Gr.8
B'nai Shalom Day School, Greensboro, North Carolina

A Whirlwind of Emotions

xviii

It takes a second for the horrible image to sink in. I see a Nazi soldier killing a mother who is holding her child. When I look at this picture, I feel a whirlwind of emotions. I am confused, regretful; I even feel spoiled about my own life. I also experience other emotions like vengeance and anger. This image is very disturbing.

Confused. I can barely understand one simple question – why, why did this happen? It doesn't make sense that millions of innocent people were tortured and killed. I have trouble conceiving of this idea because if I were Hitler, I wouldn't be able to handle the guilt of having created a plan like this.

Regretful. I have never done much to help people in need. I have donated to a few causes, but nothing more than that. Yet if I were in a homeless person's position, I would beg people to help me. So why don't we help? It's because most of us think that if we ignore the problem, it will simply go away. The truth is that it just gets bigger and bigger until it can't be ignored. Everyone ignored Hitler hoping he would stop, but he never did, and look what happened. A world war, six years, and fifty million lives later,[xix] he was stopped. We can learn from the past, and work to solve problems in politically unstable countries before they escalate out of control.

Spoiled. I live my life every day without a thought about how lucky I am. I feel safe as I walk to school. When I open my cupboards I know food will be there. Over the course of five years, those same basic rights radically changed for millions of people in Europe living under Nazi occupation. I can't imagine in my wildest dreams being ripped out of my home and sent to work as a slave to Hitler, or worse.

Vengeful. Hitler never paid for what he did. He got away by taking his own life, and never faced trial, as did some high-ranking Nazis. But I so badly want to believe that he faced the consequences for what he did. The reality is I never will be able to do anything about this. No matter how hard I try or how angry I feel, the matter will always be out of my power to control. I have learned to let it go and trust that wherever Hitler may be, he will have faced the appropriate judgment.

Graham Swarbrick, Gr.7
St. Nicholas Catholic School, Waterloo, Ontario

Simon Wiesenthal Is a Hero

Heroism is a quality that pushes a person to make a difference in the world, or do something that benefits others. For example, Simon Wiesenthal, a well-known Nazi hunter, made it his life's work to ensure that Nazi war criminals were brought to justice and that those who perished in the Holocaust were not forgotten. He once said, "The history of man is the history of crimes and history can repeat. So information is a defence."[xx] Through many years of hard work, courage and determination, Simon Wiesenthal made a remarkable difference in the world. He showed important laudable traits of a hero: determination, courage, and loyalty.

Determination is a tool that can be used to defeat discouragement; it builds character and helps one to succeed. Wiesenthal's search for wanted Nazis was arduous, and there were times when he must have felt that he was losing hope. However, he never gave up. In fact, Simon Wiesenthal continued his Nazi searches right up to his death at age 96. By that time, he had brought thousands of war criminals to justice all over the world.

Not everyone applauded his efforts, though. In 1982, a bomb planted by neo-Nazis exploded in front of his house. Even that did not stop Wiesenthal. And when tenants of his office building signed a petition forcing him to move, Wiesenthal continued his prolonged, impassioned struggle to let the world know that the Holocaust really did happen. He is quoted as saying, "Violence is like a weed; it does not die even in the greatest drought."[xxi] Even though violence may never come to an end, it is still important to work to stop it. And that's what Simon Wiesenthal spent his life doing.

Courage means having strength to stand up to others, even when it is easier to just back away. Even when his enemies put a bounty on his head – 'wanted dead, not alive' – Wiesenthal would not stop working for what he believed was right. Throughout his life, Simon Wiesenthal received hate mail and death threats. In spite of all of this he never stopped hunting down Nazis and teaching people about the Holocaust. All the intimidation in the world never held him back.

Simon Wiesenthal made many public speeches about his experience during the Holocaust. Remembering the horrific events of World War II and sharing them with the world is a hard thing to do and takes daring. Simon Wiesenthal felt it was his duty to education the younger generations since he believed the world ought to know about what happened. He once said, "For your benefit, learn from our tragedy. It is not a written law that the next victims will be the Jewish people. It can be others too."[xxii]

Loyalty is an important attribute – to never give up on a person for any reason whatsoever. Simon Wiesenthal lost eighty-nine relatives and many friends in the Holocaust. He vowed that he would always remember them. He said, "Someone had to live on for the ones who died and tell what it was really like."[xxiii] Simon Wiesenthal held on to his memories and valiantly told the world his heartbreaking account of surviving through World War II. A friend once congratulated him on his detective work and said, "If you had gone back to building houses (Simon's job before the war), you would have been a millionaire. Why didn't you?"

Wiesenthal replied, "When we come to the other world and meet the millions of Jewish people that perished in the Holocaust, they will ask us, 'What have you done?' There will be many answers...But I will say, 'I didn't forget you'..."[xxiv]

Simon Wiesenthal was one of the survivors who wanted to do all he could to make sure that a tragedy like the Holocaust would never happen again. Wiesenthal thought ahead for the next generation, and he knew there would come a time when the world might deny this time in history. Therefore, he prepared himself for that and decided to act.

Ann Zaidel, Gr.7
Yorkhill Elementary School, Thornhill, Ontario

We Can't Forget

Every single person in the world is unique. Today we praise people for being different or special. During the Holocaust millions of Jews were persecuted and killed for being different.

Can you imagine a world where all people are the same? That world would be so boring. So why did some people try to create a world without Jews? Jews are human beings like everyone. So why would others want to torture and kill us? As early as kindergarten, teachers and parents teach us the value of being kind and respectful toward other people. So why did Hitler and the Nazis not understand something that three- and four-year-olds would know?

Even though this tragedy for the Jews is over, around the world there is still persecution against people of other cultures, religions, and beliefs.

Although everyone wants to forget the tragedy that happened, how can we forget the eleven million people, six million of whom were Jewish, who died for no reason other than being different? We must remember what happened in order to keep our ancestors' spirits alive.

Robbie Goodman, Gr.6
Fieldstone Day School, Toronto, Ontario

The Power of Hate

Some time ago, our class slowly filed into a neighboring school's gym. We were met by Holocaust survivor Eva Olsson. Listening to her speech was like having a curtain open before my eyes.

The truth, no matter how horrifying, couldn't be simpler. One emotion – hate – had killed more than six million Jews. Yes, it was Hitler and his many followers who started it, who created concentration camps, and who ordered the Final Solution. But it was hate that was the driving force. It was hate for Roma, homosexuals, and especially Jews that led to their deaths.

Eva Olsson described to us the stench of burning flesh that filled the air in the concentration camps. She told us of the mass graves that were everywhere. She told us of the gas chambers that killed so many. Then, as we sat there, in a mixture of shock, anger, and sadness, tight knots in our throats and tears welling in our eyes, she told us the real cause of everything. She told us that hate did it. Hate drove the SS guards to torture the Jews. Hate drove people to lock the doors to the gas chambers. Hate drove Jews to their deaths.

More than eleven million lives were lost, six million of them Jews. We all need to know that hate can kill others again.

Derek Manderson, Gr.7
Fallingbrook Public School, Whitby, Ontario

No Life is Worth More than Another

During my trip to Israel for my Bat Mitzvah, I visited Yad Vashem, the Holocaust Memorial Museum. At Yad Vashem, I was "twinned" with a girl who was born on my birth date, but perished in the Holocaust before the age of Bat-Mitzvah. My twin's name was Rachel Kalmanowicz and I was given her deportation document to the concentration camp. She was born in Paris on February 11th, 1933. I was born on February 11th, 1997, fifty-three years after Rachel died. During the war, Rachel was brought to the Auschwitz concentration camp. She never lived to experience her Bat-Mitzvah.

My experience of being matched with Rachel was both interesting and meaningful. I learned, through my research, that she had a sister who was also deported to Auschwitz at the same time. Rachel was only eleven years old when she died there, along with her sister, in one of the deadliest concentration camps. I tried to imagine what it would be like living in those conditions, and it made me feel horrible. Rachel must have been very frightened because she was taken away from her family. I cannot imagine being separated from my parents or siblings.

I once had a dream about the Holocaust. I dreamt that my grandparents, my brother, and I were going to see a movie. Adolf Hitler was there and he was sitting near the front of the theater. All of a sudden, a spotlight shone brightly on me and my family, and we knew that the reason for this was because we were Jewish. Hitler called my brother up to the stage and killed him right in front of me. I woke up shaking with fear. Even though it was just a dream, it felt real.

It wasn't until recently that I realized the symbolism in this dream. Today, the only way we can understand the Holocaust is through survivors, pictures, and films. This is probably why the setting of my dream was a movie theater. In my dream, my parents were not with me. Rachel, my "twin", was also separated from her parents. During the Holocaust, Jewish families must have felt like they were under a spotlight and were being singled out by non-Jewish people. The spotlight in my dream symbolized Jews being targeted by the Nazis. When my brother was killed in front me, I felt despair, and anger, and hatred toward Hitler and his regime. During the Holocaust, many Jews had to witness their loved ones being murdered. It is hard to believe that my nightmare was a reality for many people.

In the past, Jews were mistreated and even killed for their beliefs. Jewish people used to have to hide the fact that they were Jewish. I take pride in my Jewish identity and know that my family and Jewish friends and teachers do as well. I am lucky to live in a society and in a time where everyone in my community is treated with respect. After the Holocaust ended, many people swore that this would never happen again. Unfortunately, there are still genocides taking place in our world today, in places like Darfur and the Sudan. I believe it is our job to try to put an end to this rather than turn a blind eye. We can help by raising awareness, raising money to help the victims, and by pressuring our governments to do something to stop the cycles of hatred.

People all over the world are different – different colors, different languages, and different beliefs. However, we are all the same because we are all human beings. We all have families, we experience emotions like love and happiness, and we are all on this earth for a purpose. No life is worth more than another.

Sami Shinder, Gr.8
Leo Baeck Day School (South Campus), Toronto, Ontario

Chapter 11

Fighting Back

Many people wonder why the Jews did not fight back against their Nazi oppressors. But was it really possible to rise up against the force of the Nazi army? The Nazi soldiers were well trained and had tanks, and endless supplies of ammunition. What could Jewish individuals possibly do in the face of such overwhelming power and force? The answer is there was a lot that Jews did to fight back.

One of the most famous acts of resistance took place in the Warsaw Ghetto. In 1943, a group of young men and women came together to form the Jewish Fighting Organization. When the Jewish prisoners of the ghetto were being deported to the Treblinka concentration camp, these brave Jewish soldiers, using a handful of guns and makeshift explosives, began to attack the Nazi guards and soldiers. Despite the overwhelming force of the Nazi army, it still took over a month to control the resistance fighters. Most of these brave young men and women were killed or deported to the camps. But many months later, there were reports of Jewish resisters still fighting from the wreckage of the Warsaw Ghetto.

There were many similar acts of resistance in concentration camps and ghettos across Europe. Some Jews who were not imprisoned in these places, formed or joined fighting units that tried to stop Nazi plans from moving forward. These fighters, or Partisans, operated in the forests surrounding cities and towns. They bombed rail lines, forged documents, and attacked Nazi units. They were instrumental in slowing down the Nazi war machinery.

Resistance during the Holocaust took many forms, not just armed combat. Many Jews found ways to maintain their self-respect and dignity, even as their rights were being taken away and they were being cruelly treated. This was known as spiritual resistance. For example, even though it was not permitted by the Nazis, many Jews in ghettos continued to create plays, music, and art. Religious services were conducted in secret. Schools were opened for Jewish children. Books were smuggled in to establish libraries. All of these activities and more were acts of resistance against Nazi control.

The truth is, there were many examples of Jews who did fight back – both from within the ghettos and concentration camps as well as from hiding places and secret locations. This chapter contains some stories that talk about acts of resistance during the Holocaust. Resistance fighters had little hope of actually succeeding against the Nazi armies. Still, their acts of defiance are an important part of the history of events during the Holocaust.

Camp Gurs

The music was like a stream; it flowed through my ears and left my mind clear and peaceful. Living in the camp was awful, but the music helped make it bearable. I closed my eyes and listened as the old man on the rickety stool played his scratched-up guitar, seemingly unaware of his desolate surroundings. A bang – the music stopped, and then chaos nearby. The Nazis were coming, and they would not be leaving empty-handed. I looked around and saw no one but the old man. He got up slowly and walked around the corner. My heart beat louder than the guns as I followed the man down an alley where he stopped and turned.

"What do you want?" he asked gruffly.

"I…I need a place to hide."

"Fine," he said, "but if they come after us, my guitar comes before you. Do you understand?"

I gulped and stepped behind a box. The man's fingers gracefully moved up and down the strings making a beautiful sound that was almost inaudible.

I mustered up my courage and asked, "Can I try?"

The man nodded, handed me the guitar, and thus started my music career. I came and sat with the man every day, to watch him play. Sometimes he would teach me things. I learned fast and he seemed impressed, but was never completely satisfied with my playing. The music made my stomach feel full and my mind cleaner. It was all I had.

"Where did you learn to play?" I asked.

The man laughed. "When will you learn, boy? No one can teach you to play. I can teach you the notes and songs, but you must learn to play on your own. And I can tell *you* that you still have much to learn."

I started to make up tunes and sing them, and soon the man let me play the entire day while he closed his eyes and listened. As I played, I thought of everything that I had been through.

The dim days and the gray meals.

The dirt and the rust.

My life full of fear, longing, and trust.

I trust the old man, old as he may be, to teach my fingers the notes and to watch over me.

I strummed a chord and finished the song. The man was getting thinner and paler. I offered him some of my food, but he always refused.

The Nazis were rounding up the elderly. I couldn't help feeling worried for the poor, sick, old man. I knew they could take him any day now, but he refused to stay hidden.

One day as I was practicing a folksong, they came. The Nazis marched in. I tried to run but I couldn't move. They came closer.

The man turned and said, "I know that you will escape, and I also know I will not live for very much longer. But rest assured that I will watch over you, and not as your teacher. I am your audience and when you play, think of me because I will be listening."

And then he was gone.

Kaelie Toone, Gr.7
Glenview Senior Public School, Toronto, Ontario

After the Uprising

During the Warsaw Ghetto uprising, hundreds of poorly armed Jewish soldiers attacked the Nazi army. The Jewish soldiers said that they had killed hundreds of Nazi soldiers, but the Nazis claimed to have only 17 dead and 93 injured. The number of Jewish deaths was much worse. The reports were that 1,300 Jews had been killed and 57,885 deported and gassed in the death camps.[xxvi] This photo shows the Nazis walking away from burning buildings in the Warsaw Ghetto. You can also see the terrible conditions in which the Jewish prisoners were forced to live.

As for the Jewish army, they had few weapons and a quarter of their recruits were barely older than children. But they still fought as hard as they could to defend their freedom. This was not a fair fight because the Nazi soldiers were heavily armed and well trained. This uprising took place in January 1943. After the fighting was over, most of the remaining Jews were sent to the death camps. A few surviving Jews hid in deserted buildings and alleyways to avoid being taken. They had ammunition and guns taken from the Nazi soldiers they had killed. With explosives, the surviving Jews were able to blow up several armored cars and kill hundreds of soldiers. The Nazis were not about to give up, and eventually they came up with another plan.

Even though they knew that there were Jewish people hiding in the buildings, they still set fire to them. In this picture, the Nazis appear very cold-hearted as they walk away from the destruction.

Connor Lobb-Macdonald, Gr.7
Glenview Senior Public School, Toronto, Ontario

Resistance

Deafening bombs hit defenceless buildings. Cries of help are answered with silence. Orders are barked by Nazi mouths. And I have to sit here and watch it all through a window. I am a Christian girl, so I do not have to suffer all of this pain. My name is Elizabeth Strauss. I moved from Austria to Amsterdam because of a job offer my father had received. My heart has now split in two; I am thankful that I am Christian, but I want to help the Jewish people. When I told my mother, she said that if I did help, I'd be shot and left for dead.

"Just be glad it's not you!" said my older brother, William. I glared at him, and then left for my room.

Mother came into my room. She sat on my bed and said, "Papa will be working very late tonight, so he won't make it for supper." I was shocked at the news, for Papa had never, ever been late for *anything* in his life, especially supper.

My mother finally told me that he was never coming home again. He had seen an SS officer beating a Jew and thought that that was not right. He tried to help, but the SS officer had a gun. So my father had been shot, and killed. From that point on, I despised the Nazis. I swore that if I had the chance, I'd destroy the Nazi army and Hitler himself. Next year I would turn eighteen. I would finally join the Resistance.

Eighteen, a good age where you become free, smart, and independent. I left for the countryside and joined the Resistance. I became a land operator with my own machine gun. My unit and I headed to Germany where we disguised ourselves as Nazis. Our mission was to infiltrate the Nazi ranks and fight from within.

Though Hitler killed himself, I still think my team and I did our job to serve the world. Never again shall anyone be racist and try to get rid of any religion. After all, we are the same people, God's people.

Elisabeth Dennis, Gr.5
Durant Rd. Elementary School, Raleigh, North Carolina

Walls

If we don't remember, what will be left?
If the library is burned, what will we learn?
If the honor is broken, will lies break free?
If the sword's work is forgotten, who will defend?
If the dead aren't buried, who will teach?
If the fences are cut, what will keep the memories in?
If the clothes are dumped, will identities be lost?
If the barracks fall, what will show us the pain?
If the black is erased, will only yellow and red remain?
If the numbers disappear, who will believe?
If the Holy Land is taken, where will they go?
If the evil is reborn, how will we survive?
If we forget, will the end be near?
If we build walls, it is blood we will see...

Vincent Noh, Gr.8
Fieldstone Day School, Toronto, Ontario

Chapter 12

We Are Their Voice

Have you ever heard a survivor of the Holocaust tell his or her story? Those who have heard a survivor speak often describe this as one of the most meaningful moments of his or her life. There is something so personal and emotional about hearing the words spoken by someone who has actually lived through the pain. It's the kind of experience that can stay with you forever.

We are fortunate that there are still survivors alive today who are willing to speak about this time in history. But that will not always be the case. More than sixty-five years have passed since the end of the Second World War. Many survivors are already gone, and those still with us are aging. It will not be long before we lose them, too. And when they have died, all first person accounts of this time in history will have died with them. Now more than ever, we need to preserve these voices of history.

And we need to know that by remembering what survivors have gone through, we are honoring them and their experiences.

"To forget the dead would be akin to killing them a second time." That's something that the noted historian and author, Elie Wiesel once said. Born in Romania, Wiesel was deported to Auschwitz in 1944. He endured over eight months in horrifying conditions, and managed to survive. After the war he became a journalist and wrote more than fifty books, of which the most well-known is *Night*,[16] based on his experiences in Auschwitz as well as Buna and Buchenwald concentrations camps. He was awarded the Nobel Peace Prize in 1986. In awarding the prize, the Nobel committee referred to Wiesel as a "messenger to mankind."

Think about the stories that you will read in this chapter, and other stories that you will find in the future. Remember them. Record them. Retell them. Tell your own. You can be the voice of this history.

---

[16] Wiesel, Elie. *Night*, page xv, New York: Hill & Wang, 1972. Print.

A Room Full of Names

There is a room at the Holocaust Memorial Museum in Toronto that has names on plaques that are hung on its circular wall. These are the names of one million people who were murdered in the Holocaust.

When I first walked into this room, I thought I was going to burst into tears because the names of one million murdered Holocaust victims surrounded me. I think this is exactly why the room is circular. When I was surrounded by the names of real people, the full reality of the Holocaust finally hit me. Not only was I devastated that all these people no longer lived, I was also furious, grateful, and ashamed all at the same time. Furious at everyone who thought killing, torturing, and starving so many human beings was okay. And furious at Adolf Hitler and his followers who killed so many people. I was grateful, because unlike the people on this wall, I have a living, wonderful family, enough food and shelter, and I am alive. These are all precious privileges that these people had taken away from them for no reason at all. I am ashamed, because members of the same human race to which I belong thought it was all right to treat other humans like animals, to put them in concentration camps, to give them little or no food and water at all, and to murder them in brutal and unforgivable ways. I will never be able to fully explain all the emotions I felt in this room. That is how powerful the experience was.

There are not only adult names on this wall; there are also names of children: six-year-olds, nine-year-olds, even three-year-olds. These children were never able to grow up, get married, or have children of their own; they were stripped of their lives and their childhood. These children experienced things that no child should have to bear. What was supposed to be their childhood was not a childhood at all, but rather a wretched nightmare.

The plaques in this room are not only there to remind us of all the people who were lost in the Holocaust, but they are also there for their families. When someone you love passes away, you can always visit their grave. But there are no graves for the people on this wall. Their bodies were burned into nothing but ashes. Their names are here in this small, circular room where they can be visited by their loved ones.

This room is also here to remind us of how tragic the Holocaust was so that we do everything in our power to prevent such a monstrous, horrible event from happening again. Even though the circular room is full of hate, sadness, and longing, it helps us to never forget what happened in 1939 through 1945. We cannot afford to forget.

Katie Dzyngel, Gr.7
Eagle Ridge Public School, Ajax, Ontario

A Future Denied

When I look at this photo of shoes displayed at the Auschwitz museum it is distressing to see that it represents an overwhelming loss of life. I cannot believe how many people were murdered for their faith and culture!

It makes me feel sad and infuriated at the same time just thinking about how one race of human beings could kill another race without even thinking about their actions. How anyone could be so cruel, I will never know.

When the Russians arrived in Auschwitz on January 25th, 1945, they found piles of clothes and shoes that numbered in the hundreds of thousands. I wonder how so many people could have been murdered that way. The idea that the Nazis treated these people worse than they would treat animals is horrifying to me. I am a person who believes that everyone should be treated with respect and fairness.

Since some of these shoes belonged to children, it makes me wonder what they might have grown up to be – teachers, doctors, engineers, lawyers, electricians? If the children had survived and become teachers, they could have educated their students about the Holocaust. If they had become doctors, they could have found the cures to numerous fatal diseases. By becoming lawyers, they could have helped bring justice to lots of clients. These children could have changed the world. We'll never know what they were capable of. Tragically, their lives were snuffed out along with all of their hopes, dreams, and chances for the future.

There are shoes from every age group in the pile, and I'm sure that the parents who were in the concentration camps had hopes for their children that were never realized. These parents would never see their children's first days of school, celebrate any more of their birthdays, play any more games with them, or tell them that they loved them ever again.

There were also grandparents in the concentration camps. It must have been awful as their children and grandchildren, whom they loved and had hopes for, were being killed. There would no longer be any family dinners or baking cookies. How painful this must have been!

For all of the children out there, imagine losing your parents. How would you feel? I know that I would be devastated. And for all of the parents out there, imagine losing your children. How would you feel? Those horrible feelings were experienced by Jewish families in the Holocaust. There are still people today who are racist and feel that they are superior to others. These people must stop their negative views. If not, history is doomed to repeat itself.

People in my generation may be the ones to create another horrible event like the Holocaust. We could be responsible for creating World War III. I hope those in my generation will strive to accept others, and respect themselves enough to realize that we are all the same. We all have hopes and dreams, and we all have the ability to love – our most important trait. We are all human beings sharing one planet, and if only we could all respect each other, no lives would be lost through war and disagreements. All lives are meaningful.

Juliana Harris, Gr.8
LaSalle Public School, LaSalle, Ontario

Reflections on Judith

I met Judith Rubinstein on Sunday, February 6, 2011, at the Terraces of Baycrest in Toronto. I had read books about the Holocaust such as *Daniel's Story,*[xxviii] *Clara's War,*[xxix] and *Hana's Suitcase*[xxx] before I met Judith. However, meeting a real survivor who had lived through the Holocaust was an experience like no other. Judith shared her stories with so much passion and generosity.

Judith Rubinstein was born in Szerinch, Hungary in 1920. She grew up with her parents and three younger brothers. Judith was only 24 years of age in 1944 when the Nazis invaded Hungary. All the Jewish people of Hungary were forced to wear a yellow star on their clothing so that they could be identified as Jews, and persecuted.

On May 20 1944, Judith, her family, and others from her city were put on a train for two days and taken to a ghetto in a place called Ujhel. Eventually she ended up in Auschwitz, where she saw the evil Dr. Josef Mengele who was directing people from the train to two separate lines – one for those who looked strong and could be put to work, and the other for those who were destined for the gas chamber. Judith's family was separated from her. Her mother saved Judith's life by pushing her to the other line with four young girls who looked strong, so that she could survive. That was the last time Judith saw her family. She heard from others that before people were led to the gas chambers, they were made to strip and their hair was shaved off. Cruelly, their hair was gathered and sent to Germany to stuff mattresses. As the smoke came out of the chimney from the crematorium, the Nazis would taunt Judith and say, "Look, that smoke is your mother." The ashes of the burnt bodies were spread across the fields and used as fertilizer.

Judith was stripped and given a uniform. She was not allowed to wear underwear. Her head was shaved. She was put to work with others for endless periods of time. This continued until the war was over in 1945. Judith got married and moved to Italy until 1948 when she and her husband moved to Canada.

As I heard Judith's story, I felt sadness and anger. I felt angry at Hitler and thought he was a sick person with a sick mind. I could not imagine that one individual could have the power to order others to take the lives of six million Jewish people. I could not imagine what it must have been like to be separated from your family, and to know that the people you loved most were being taken to death camps to die.

When I met Judith, I was amazed to see an actual survivor talk about what she had gone through. As I was listening to her stories, I was reflecting on my own life and wondering, "What if my grandparents went through the same thing? What if I was a Jew and I had to go through the torture? Could I have had the same faith as Judith?" Judith's faith really impressed me when she told me, "I believe in God. Everyone is God's child. Be respectful, and love everyone." How remarkable and how strong she is!

I lost my own grandmother on New Year's Eve 2011. Judith reminded me of her in many ways. Not only is she close to my granny's age, she has a granddaughter named Alyshah, which is my name. Amazingly, the name that Judith used for her granddaughter is the pet name my family uses for me – "Looshoo-Leeshee." In so many ways, I was comforted to be in Judith's presence, and happy to know that she had maintained her strong faith in goodness, despite her experience. I was relieved to hear that she has a wonderful family of two children, nine grandchildren, and many great-grandchildren. She shares her vivid stories so that children like me can learn about the Holocaust. She generously offered to see me again, should I want to know more.

I am most grateful to have met Judith Rubinstein. She taught me a lot – mostly how to keep faith and hope, and re-build a life, even after going through the catastrophic experience of the Holocaust. She also taught me that we should never forget that time in history, and that learning about it is one way to ensure that it will never happen again!

Alyshah Velji, Gr.7
Eagle Ridge Public School, Ajax, Ontario

Learning from the Past

The Holocaust is something people should never forget! It showed us that even though God created everyone equal, terrible things can still happen when people do not respect this.

In 1933, a man named Adolf Hitler gained power in Germany and wanted all Jews to be eliminated. He thought that Jews were evil and that they were the reason Germany had lost the First World War. I think Hitler was angry about this defeat and he tried to find somebody to blame. Unfortunately, for the innocent Jewish people, he picked them.

Hitler must have had a warped mind because what he did to the Jewish people was unthinkable and horrific. He killed so many Jews (children and adults), that they were almost wiped out completely in Europe. But before he killed them, he made their lives miserable. When they were still in their towns, he created laws that would prevent them from associating with non-Jewish people. He wouldn't let them into public places and shops, and children were not allowed to go to school. Eventually they were sent to concentration camps where they were fed only once a day if they were lucky, and the food was inedible. Jewish prisoners had to live in crowded barracks, sharing the space with hundreds of others. This was cruel punishment and unbearable for the Jewish prisoners.

If I were a survivor, I might feel extremely lucky that I had not been killed along with so many. But then I would think about my family, relatives, and friends who were not so lucky. The survivors felt as if a part of themselves died along with their loved ones.

The Holocaust is known all over the world as a horrendous crime against society. But for some reason, similar crimes are still happening today. In Rwanda, the military was told to get rid of certain groups of people, in a policy known as "ethnic cleansing." The same thing happened in Bosnia where the Serbians and Croatians killed each other.

In religion class, I have learned about human dignity, and how everyone deserves to be valued as a person, to be loved, and to be included. Hitler did not show any of these innocent people any kind of respect. He did not value the Jews. He made sure that they were not included by isolating them from the rest of society. But they were loved by the people who cared about them – their family and friends. Hitler could not take that from them!

I know that this was a sad time in world history. But we have to think about and learn from the past. This will, hopefully, make the world a better place. I hope that in my lifetime I will see the end of such horrific crimes as genocide and ethnic cleansing. We can only hope for a more peaceful, compassionate, and understanding world.

Jack Madjeruh, Gr.7
Regina Mundi Catholic School, Hamilton, Ontario

Why Remember?

Why remember?

Why do we remember the Allied soldiers? We should always remember the soldiers because many were drafted into the war, though many also volunteered. They put their lives on the line to fight for our freedom. They gave us rights, rights that the Jews who were killed never had. Many soldiers made it back home to their families. But many did not. That's why everybody should remember and respect these people for risking their lives to help protect us.

Why do we remember the Jewish people? We remember them and all of those tragic and horrible events because nobody should live under those circumstances. No one deserves to be killed because of their faith. The Jews were put into concentration camps and were starved, poisoned, or shot. That was a dreadful time, and we are grateful to live in a country that has rights that they did not have. It's sad to say that during the Holocaust, over eleven million people perished – not only Jews but many others as well.

Why should we remember Adolf Hitler, the man who did these terrible things to the Jews? He had power and he controlled his whole Nazi army, which almost wiped out an entire race.

We should remember the Jews, the soldiers, and Hitler. If we don't look back at history, we're doomed to repeat it.

Sean Muir, Gr.6
Harmony Heights Public School, Oshawa, Ontario

Message from Behind the Wire

xxxi

These are the children of the Holocaust. The boy in the front row, toward the right, is wearing the Star of David, a sign of being Jewish. The children look cold, confused, and scared. They are trapped like animals and do not know why. Even if they could escape, they have nowhere to go. The Nazi soldiers rounded up any Jewish people they could find. To the Nazis, the Jews were the enemy and had to be destroyed. They didn't care if their victims were children, and especially didn't worry about separating them from their parents. Their parents would die anyway.

The concentration camps were full of these children. Most of them were killed instantly, while some worked until they died. Many died from diseases in the camp. The only comfort they had was one another. They huddled together for warmth, and the older ones tried to help the younger ones survive. We don't know what happened to many of these children. We will never know. This is a tragic piece of history. It is important that we don't forget this tragedy. Even if it makes us feel sad or uncomfortable, we must remember it.

Christina Sanidas, Gr.7
Eagle Ridge Public School, Ajax, Ontario

The Devil's Arithmetic — a Reflection

The Devil's Arithmetic[xxxii] by Jane Yolen tells the experience of Hannah, a girl who is sick and tired of remembering the past and more focused on the here and now. However, all that changes when she is transported back to World War II and the Holocaust. To her horror she learns that she is no longer Hannah, but Chaya, a girl gifted with memories from the future.

I can't say I *enjoyed* this book, but I will say that I respected it. I didn't like the descriptions of the killings, but I can finally grasp and comprehend the fear that people experienced in the Holocaust and the way in which Jews were treated. My favorite part in this novel was when Chaya/Hannah tricked a Nazi soldier into believing that she was her friend, Rivkah. Chaya/Hannah was finally able to do what she wanted to do from the beginning – change the outcome of the future. By giving up her life, she saved one Jew from the horror of the gas chambers.

I feel this book is meant for an audience of twelve to fifteen-year-olds. Younger children might be disturbed by some of the graphic information. I would only recommend this book to my friends who are mature enough to understand and read it.

I would definitely be pleased to read another book by this author. Her style of writing kept my interest. I cried when Chaya/Hannah cried and laughed when she laughed.

Rebecca Turner, Gr.6
Jewish People's and Peretz School (JPPS), Montreal, Quebec

The Other Side of the Fence

It's January 27, 1946, late in the afternoon in Berlin, Germany. My name is Isabella Muller and I'm nineteen years old. As I sit here on the windowsill and gaze at the ruins of Berlin, I can't help but think back thirteen years ago, when the horrific events first began. I was only six years old.

In 1933, the government changed when Adolf Hitler came to power in Germany. He made my parents believe that what he was doing was right, but I wasn't so sure. When I went to school, I wasn't allowed to sit with my best friend, Rosa, because she was Jewish. She had to change schools and I didn't see her for a very long time. Jewish people weren't allowed outside at night, and eventually many were shipped away from Berlin. The first question that came to mind was why Rosa would be treated this way when she did nothing wrong.

By 1934, Hitler had gained total control of Germany, and I often wondered what had happened to my friend, Rosa. My father was sent to Dachau to work, so my family had to move. We moved in late 1940 when I was 13 years old and this war was already well underway. As we settled into our new home, there was a different feeling to this place.

Every time I went outside there was a disgusting smell and dark, thick clouds in the sky. My parents didn't say anything, so I acted as if nothing was wrong. However, I could see barbed wire and a big building with smoke coming out of it. I sneaked out the next day to take a closer look. People were everywhere, either marching, working, or just sitting around. Everyone looked the same, dressed in striped uniforms, and all of them were very skinny. I looked closer and my heart dropped. On the other side of the barbed wire fence was Rosa, my best friend from Berlin. She didn't look very well. She saw me and tried to talk, but our conversation was cut short when a soldier approached her. I was terrified. Without a word, he shot her in the back of the head, and pointed the gun at me. I ran as fast as I could, never looking back.

I begged my parents to take me back to Berlin, but they refused. Over the next three years, Russian, Canadian, and the United States armies entered Germany, and the war ended. Adolf Hitler committed suicide in his bunker in Berlin in 1945, and that's when I knew it was finally over.

It's been thirteen years since everything in Germany changed. I witnessed only a tiny portion of what happened during the Holocaust. But the experience made me grow up. There were eleven million people who suffered during that time, six million of them Jews, like my friend, Rosa. The main question in Germany after the Holocaust was "How will we remember?" Some strive to treat all people equally; others have helped restart the lives of those who suffered in the Holocaust. For me, and many other people in Germany, I just think about what it would have been like to be a victim.

Emma Sweet, Gr.8
Minesing Central School, Minesing, Ontario

Teach the World

The Holocaust. The name brings to mind images of men, women, and children laboring in work camps, and the genocide of the Jews of Europe. Mostly Jews were rounded up and forced to be the prisoners of cruel Nazi officials. The Holocaust was triggered by the actions of one man, Adolf Hitler, along with his followers. In some ways, I feel connected to the Holocaust because I'm Jewish. But I also feel that all people, even if they are not Jewish, should know about the Holocaust. We have to keep talking about this time in history, and keep passing the knowledge on, so that future generations know enough to stop dictators like Hitler from ever rising to power again.

Knowledge of the Holocaust can be learned through books, documentaries, and real-life stories from Holocaust survivors. I don't know, and hopefully never will know, what it was like to be in the concentration camps. But talking to Holocaust survivors is one way to better comprehend the suffering experienced by these people. Although a lot of Holocaust survivors may not want to talk about their experiences, those who do can teach us a lot about this time.

In learning about the Holocaust, I feel we should understand exactly why Hitler condemned the Jews. Hitler's fanatical ideas were that Jews weren't "pure" Germans, so they shouldn't exist as they could "contaminate" those who were. I wonder if this idea was a result of Germany's earlier defeat in World War I. Hitler may have imagined that this defeat was caused by German Jews who he claimed had weakened the country. This is what he stated, though of course it was completely false. This is an area that I need to learn more about, so I can better understand why the Holocaust happened. This is important for us in order to be able to resist a similar situation in the future, and perhaps stop it from happening again.

I have a good life here in Canada, and it is often hard to feel connected to what happened in the Holocaust. However, the Holocaust is an important event to teach and learn about. It is our responsibility to teach about what happened in the Holocaust as a lesson to the world.

Elan Yaphe, Gr.6B
Downtown Jewish Community School, Toronto, Ontario

We Are Their Voice

The meaning of the word Holocaust is "massive destruction, especially by fire." It has also come to mean the genocide of six million Jews during World War II. During that terrible period, which lasted from the time the Nazis came to power until the end of the Second World War (1933–1945), millions of people were victimized and murdered. Jews were forced to leave their homes and were taken to concentration camps to be used as forced laborers. Others were taken to death camps where they were killed in gas chambers. Many died from starvation, disease, and torture. The Nazis did not spare anyone – men, women, children, and babies were murdered. The Nazis killed Jews in massive numbers for absolutely no reason at all.

Although it is very difficult to learn about this time in history, I think it is important for every person to know about this horrifying event. If we don't educate ourselves and others about the Holocaust, it is possible for history to repeat itself.

My Saba[17] Chaim (my late grandfather) was a Holocaust survivor. He was only thirteen years old when the war broke out, and he spent most of his teenage years trying to survive. He was taken to Auschwitz concentration camp and was separated from his family there. He was forced to work, but the others were all sent to the gas chambers. My grandfather was in Auschwitz for three years, and then was forced on the death march from Auschwitz in Poland, all the way to Buchenwald in Germany. The Nazis were attempting to escape from the Allied forces. If prisoners stopped, tripped, fell, or could not walk anymore, they were shot on the spot. Once in Buchenwald, my grandfather was put to work again until the camp was liberated by the American army in April 1945. After the liberation, my grandfather moved to Israel. There, he met my grandmother and they married. They had four daughters named Tzippi, Tami, Ruth, and Aviva. My Saba named his children after his family members who were lost in the Holocaust. The only evidence left of his family is two photographs taken before the war started that he had with

---

[17] Hebrew for grandfather

him during the Holocaust. When I look at these photos, it makes me feel as if a part of me is missing. I feel sad to know that my mother never got to know her grandparents and her family on her father's side. It makes me angry to know that so many lives were destroyed and tragically changed forever because of hatred, racism, and anti-Semitism.

I feel as if a part of me was taken away when Hitler and his followers killed all those families of Jews, including mine. I feel a connection between myself and the people who died in this horrific time. We must keep the stories of the Holocaust alive. We must continue to tell the stories of survivors. When they are gone, we are their voice!

Ori Berman, Gr.8
Leo Baeck Day School (North Campus), Toronto, Ontario

Amelia Zhang, Gr.8
Fieldstone Day School, Toronto, Ontario

Chapter 13

Putting Words into Actions

So what happens now?

How do we take the writing that young people like you have created and turn it into something even more effective? How do we become positive voices for the future? There are many things that you can do.

The first important step is to keep learning about the Holocaust and other genocides, and to think critically about the events that occurred. Why did these massacres happen? Who was involved? Who cooperated? Who fought back? Amazingly, there are those who say that these events did not happen. The more you discover about history, the better able you will be to combat these claims. We must all take an active role in opposing those who deny the Holocaust, wherever they may be.

Secondly, we need to look inward, at ourselves. We must fight against our own prejudices (and we all have them) if we are ever to contribute to the world in a positive way. We are never going to wipe out hatred; there are still too many examples of genocides in the world. Many of you will be familiar with the tragic events in Armenia, Rwanda, Cambodia, and Darfur, to name but a few. But we can start by thinking about how we as individuals can become more compassionate to those who are different from us.

Speaking up when injustice occurs is the next thing we need to be able to do. We need to find the courage to speak up against the cruelty and crimes in our communities, from name-calling and exclusion to discrimination, bullying, and homophobia, etc. We must also take a stand against war and violence that is occurring in other countries.

Small commitments can lead to bigger actions. Many of those who wrote stories for this collection said that they had learned so much just from this writing; that they were determined to do better deeds in their schools and communities. You too can join in, and be a positive voice for the future. Here are some stories that raise the banner of justice high.

Freedom

Throughout history, humankind has slaughtered, tortured, killed, and raped mercilessly. Unfortunately, we have not yet learned from these events. The Holocaust happened seventy years ago. In this horrifying massacre, the Nazis were responsible for eleven million deaths; six million victims were Jews. The devastating fact is that most of these innocent people never imagined that such a thing could ever happen to them.

Fortunately, I haven't experienced torture first hand, but in 2009 I started to understand the true meaning of freedom. During that summer, the people of my home country of Iran gained the courage to stand up against the Iranian government. I watched as family members and close friends roamed the street, asking for freedom, something that was rightfully theirs. Only after witnessing my friend take a bullet through the head did I choose to stand up and be heard. I created signs and posted them around the streets of Tehran, hoping for change. I now realize how grateful I am to be living in a free country like Canada.

Since 1939, there have been dozens of genocides in the world including ones in Rwanda, Uganda, Sierra Leone, and North Korea. Even today, the Islamic leaders of Sudan are murdering their own civilians for peaceful anti-government demonstrations. So the message the world is sending is that after seventy years, we, as "intellectually advanced" human beings, are still unable to stop prejudice and killing.

Our only hope to stop this international crisis is to care for one another as though we are all brothers and sisters, and to respect each other's beliefs. Not everyone shares the same point of view, but we must not discriminate. Rather than simply watching, we must stand up for everyone's rights and help those in need. If we don't act soon, history will repeat itself. Losing freedom is like losing blood. When we bleed, we must act quickly to stop the flow!

Arshia Eshtiagi, Gr.7
Thornhill Public School, Thornhill, Ontario

Learning from the Holocaust

About a year and a half ago, if you had asked me what the Holocaust was, I would have likely said, "Some kind of war where bad things happened." That would have been the only answer I could have given, simply because I really did not know much about it. Today though, I realize the Holocaust was an event so horrendous and indescribable, it is nearly impossible to put into words.

The first project I did on the Holocaust was for school a year ago, after our class read *The Silver Sword* by Ian Serraillier.[xxxiii] It was extremely difficult for me. As I began my research, I came across images that were almost unbearable to look at. I was very upset at how the people were treated in the concentration camps. Jews had scarcely enough food to live on; they were shot on the spot if they were not working hard enough, burned to death or sent to the gas chambers for no reason.

I can only wonder about the pain and misery these people had to endure, waiting there, day after day, night after night, wondering if they would ever be saved. People lived with the ever-constant fear of not surviving.

There are those who survived the Holocaust and those who did not. I admire both. I know that the people who did not survive didn't leave without a fight; many fought for their own lives, while some of them gave their lives freely for someone they loved. I think they are true heroes. To those who did survive, the amazing will to stay alive carried them through. I doubt I would have been one of those.

You sometimes see people on television who are tattooed with the Nazi swastika. It scares me that there are still people who agree with what Hitler said, did, and stood for. There are even some kids my age who think this is funny. They make jokes which are hard to listen to. I find it very disrespectful to those who have lived through this nightmare. Hitler began his whole campaign based on his hatred of a religion and people who were not like him, namely the Jews.

The Holocaust was a very dark period of history that should not and cannot be forgotten. If it is, then something like bullying, which can be seen by some as harmless, if left unchecked, could lead to similar disasters. Come to think of it, I am glad I learned about the Holocaust. Now, as young as I am, I can help it from happening again. I think we can all do this if we just stop for a moment, think about the Holocaust, and take it as a lesson as to how far hatred can actually go.

Rebecca Howie, Gr.8
Riverview Middle School, Riverview, New Brunswick

Not Just Some Page in a History Book

What does the Holocaust really mean to us today? Are we truly aware of what it was, or what it was like to live in that time? Can we fully understand how such a tragedy occurred, and the lessons that must be learned?

The Holocaust is difficult for my generation to comprehend. It's hard to imagine that such an enormous tragedy happened almost eighty years ago. I was shocked when I was first taught that six million Jews were murdered. But what are six million deaths? This number is so massive that it is almost incomprehensible. When a person we know or had a connection with passes away, we feel for the person. However, six million deaths are so many that in my mind it becomes a statistic or just a number. Perhaps that is why it's so difficult for us to understand. But there is a way we can change this. Schools do not spend a lot of time educating students about the Holocaust, so it's difficult for us to learn everything that happened. But each one of us can use our own initiative to do research and find more information. This will help us to better understand these important events.

Human instinct is such that we never want to learn about a dark subject. In fact, we usually want to forget the dreadful things that happen to us. In addition, there are few survivors left today for us to talk to, and there will be even fewer as time goes on. So if it's difficult for our generation, how much harder will it be for the next generation to understand, and the one after that?

We have many privileges here in Canada and can't imagine that such an evil act could have occurred, and that no one stopped it until it was too late. When Adolf Hitler came to power in Germany, many

Jewish people fled the country in fear. But they were turned away from neighboring countries. These countries did not believe that such bad things could be happening to Jews, and they did not want to be overrun with Jewish refugees. When the Nazis began restricting Jewish rights, most Jews became isolated and completely helpless. This is just like the way bullying happens in schools today. When a bully has power and no bystander steps up to confront the bully, horrible things can happen. As Edmund Burke said, "All that is necessary for evil to triumph is for good men to do nothing."[xxxiv] Although the Holocaust was on a much bigger scale, essentially the idea is the same.

But even in those dark times, there were some brave people who tried to stand up against the evil. These people risked everything to save Jews across Europe. Some of those people also died, joining the six million who perished, but their stories show us that there can be good in the world. As Anne Frank wrote, "In spite of everything, I still believe that people are truly good at heart."[xxxv]

Remembering the Holocaust is an extremely important part, not only of our lives today, but of our future. We must learn from these unimaginable tragedies because, as George Santayana stated, "Those who cannot remember the past are doomed to repeat it."[xxxvi] The Holocaust also teaches us of bravery, courage, hope, and the power of good in our world to fight evil. We might never fully know what happened during the Holocaust or feel what is was like at that time, but we can still try to understand. That is the least we can do to make sure the Holocaust won't be just some page in a history textbook.

Jerry Kim, Gr.8
Jack Chambers Public School, London, Ontario

Looking for Answers

It's hard to imagine that some Jews were able to live after the slaughter of the Holocaust. Imagine having everything taken away from you in an instant. And this happened to people who thought they were citizens of their own countries and would never be hurt. I can't imagine how Adolf Hitler could have committed such a crime. Did you know that the Jews in the camps were not allowed to help other Jews who had fallen? If they did, they would be killed. Despite this, it is amazing that some Jews had the courage to help each other even when their own lives were at risk. It is very important to learn the lessons of the Holocaust so that history does not repeat itself. Sadly, wars continue to happen. Wasting thousands and thousands of lives is senseless.

Benjamin Franklin once said, "If everyone is thinking alike, then no one is thinking."[xxxvii] If everyone is thinking of going to war, then people need to think harder. That way, we could find a civilized way to solve conflicts. If you think about the positives and negatives of war, you will find many more negative things. It's important to expand your view of the problem and look for solutions.

Francis H. Taylor, Gr.5
Durant Rd. Elementary School, Raleigh, North Carolina

The Craving to be Free

Since 1945, there have been major genocides and dozens of massacres. The world has not made much progress in terms of peace, and more countries are developing nuclear weapons. Education levels are increasing, but hatred and war have remained. History appears doomed to repeat itself.

There are many recent examples of prejudice in today's world. Statistics show that anti-Semitism is at a higher level now than it has ever been.[xxxviii] Recently, three synagogues in Montréal, Canada were vandalized by Neo-Nazis. That is not unlike the events of *Kristallnacht* in Germany in 1938.

In 1935, European Jews became targets of persecution, and eventually victims under the reign of Adolf Hitler. Six million Jews became six million fatalities; five million other people – Jehovah's Witnesses, homosexuals, mentally and physically disabled people, Roma (gypsies), and many others joined the ashes of the concentration camps. Over the years, not just the Jewish culture has been targeted, but nearly every culture has witnessed acts of hatred. Rwanda's people were victims of a mass genocide in 1994. Bosnian Serb Forces led an ethnic cleansing campaign in 1992-95. The world has watched on countless occasions as millions of people have been slaughtered on several continents. All these acts are tied to the same root – enmity or hatred. Shedding innocent blood does not solve anything.

Even though there are unremitting patterns of hatred, crisis, and war, there is a longing in most people's hearts to achieve change. In order for change to happen, we must educate the new generations in a different way. If my generation could be educated to find solutions of peace, harmony, and unity, then we would all grow up in a world filled with those things. If we could all work towards a common purpose, we would accomplish the goal of peace.

Some people believe that violence only produces more violence. If you storm into a crowd of protesters with a squad of tanks, it may silence them for the moment. But they may rise again. However, if you look for compromise or ways to solve the problem peacefully, you will gain more than you would have by using violence. Many governments have resolved twice as many issues with peace and talks than they would have by going to war.

It is in everyone's best interest to stop prejudice. If we are willing to look for solutions, we can change. In the words of Martin Luther King Jr., "Darkness cannot drive out darkness; only light can do that. Hate cannot drive out hate; only love can do that."[xxxix]

Ari Forman, Gr.7
Thornhill Public School, Thornhill, Ontario

Anna Prust, Gr.8
Forest Hill Public School, Midhurst, Ontario

Dear Esther

I found your letter of reflection on the Internet, the one you shared when you turned ninety-seven years old. The story about your life during the Holocaust deeply affected me, so I wanted to write to you. I wish to praise you for your courage and strength.

I can't believe the information you revealed. You were forced to live with five hundred women and girls in one barrack. It was extremely crowded and unsanitary. There was no heat. You had to get up at five a.m. and be at roll call by six. There you waited for hours, no matter what the weather conditions. You worked as a slave laborer in the factory, making bullets for German soldiers. You had no possessions, only clothing that came from someone who died. You lined up for hours to wash your clothes in the single sink. You had no showers and no sheets for your bed. You were starving and had only one piece of bread for eight days. Your family members were taken, never to be seen again. You knew that they were prisoners, and then found out that they had been tortured and killed in the most terrible way. It isn't any wonder people were hiding to escape being found and taken to work camps. These weren't work camps; they were death camps. You had no idea what you did to deserve this treatment, and wondered all the time when it was going to end. You fought to find a reason to stay alive. It's all so unbelievable, but it's all true.

To find out more about the Holocaust, I decided to watch the movie *The Diary of Anne Frank*,[xl] At the end of the film I tried to tell myself it was just a movie, but I know that's not true. It upset me so much I found myself crying. It scared me more than I have ever felt before to know that something like this happened. And for what reason? Kids my age have no idea about this kind of horror. I pray that we never will.

Recently, I saw in the news that the amount of money being given to Holocaust survivors and their heirs has been increased to assist those who need help and to support educational and memorial activities. There are also efforts to locate and return assets. It will never make up for the way you were forced to live or the possessions that were taken from you, the families that were lost or tortured to death. We all should be ashamed of what happened, and stop at nothing to help those of you who lived through this. That you were able to endure all this and survive to tell these truths is amazing.

I'm glad that you and others have found the strength to share your stories. I cannot imagine how painful it must have been to re-live these events. The things that you have gone through will never go away; they are with you forever. You are a remarkable person. It is through sharing your story that others are able to learn the truth – a truth that should never be forgotten. I wish to express my thanks to you for sharing with others in order that we may learn from mistakes of the past.

Your story has made me appreciate the things I have in my life, things that many in my generation take for granted: family, freedom to live as we please, and freedom of expression. The events of your life, the lives of others who lived through this, as well as those who did not survive, will stay with me forever.

Kayla Paquette, Gr.8
Jack Chambers Public School, London, Ontario

Doing the Right Thing
(The Danger of Bullying)

xli

At first glance, I didn't think much about the picture. I just thought it was an image of a Jewish man lying on the ground with Nazis standing around him. Then I looked closer and saw how truly frightening it was. I realized that the Nazis surrounding him were sneering and laughing, resembling a group of felines playing with their prey before mercilessly destroying it. I wonder how it is possible for a human being to experience feelings of joy like this, to laugh at another human's suffering and humiliation. I know that the Nazis were able to do this partially because they thought of Jews as worthless and impure, with no right to live. But what normal person can find pleasure in another's suffering?

The Nazis were not the only ones to inflict suffering on others. I see this kind of behavior almost every day at school, though these incidents are far less severe. Even so, this bullying treatment is doled out to groups of people who are *selected*, just like Jews were selected in the Holocaust. The students who are targeted at my school may look slightly different, have a quieter attitude or may belong to a different religion. In other words, just as the Jews were seen as inferior, these people in my school are seen as imperfect. They are used as toys for the amusement of those who are causing the suffering. How do some humans find it so easy to dehumanize others without feelings of guilt? To me, it seems impossible. The strongest feeling that I had while viewing the photo was guilt, for all of the times I had put down someone of less value in my eyes. I felt sorrow for all the people who have had or will go through any type of pain at the hands of others. And I felt anger, along with a deep need to protect and defend all those who have suffered. I was appalled that people like me or my fellow classmates could possibly demean another fellow human being!

So the next time I have the urge to tease or put someone down I will think of this picture. I will remember all the feelings of anger and hate I have developed toward those laughing, smug figures. Then I will ask myself, "Do I really want to act like those I despise?" I will think of this picture and decide to do the right thing when it is time. I can only hope that I have convinced anyone reading this to do the same.

Cayley McAllister, Gr.8
Eugene Reimer Middle School, Abbotsford, British Columbia

Glossary

Allied Soldiers/Allies: the countries who fought against Germany in World War II: the United States, Canada, Britain, France, and the Soviet Union.

Anti-Semitism: systematic prejudice against Jewish people.

Auschwitz: a series of Nazi concentration and death camps located near the town of Oświęcim in Poland. More than three million people were murdered there between 1942 and 1944, the majority being European Jews. Auschwitz II–Birkenau, the extermination camp, was instrumental in carrying out the Final Solution (see below).

Bat/Bar Mitzvah: a ceremony that takes place when Jewish children are 12 years old (for girls) and 13 (for boys). It marks their introduction into the Jewish adult community and acknowledges their moral and religious duties.

Bystanders: those who do nothing to stop injustices occurring around them. During the Holocaust, many bystanders obeyed the laws and ignored the growing threats to Jews, hoping to escape the consequences of Nazi terror.

Camp Gurs: a concentration camp built in 1939 in southwestern France, which originally served to confine political prisoners. Beginning in 1940, it was also used to imprison Jews, mostly of German descent, who were not French citizens. Living conditions in the camp were terrible with shortages in water, food, and clothing. Many died of diseases such as typhoid fever and dysentery. Between 1942 and 1943, Jewish prisoners were deported to death camps in Poland.

Chanukah/Hanukkah: an eight-day Jewish holiday also known as the Festival of Lights. It is a holiday of remembrance, commemorating the reclaiming, in 165 BCE, of the Jewish Temple located in Judah, modern day Israel. At that time, Jews came from all over Judah to worship at the Temple until the Syrian-Greek emperor demanded they abandon their religion and culture. Judah and his four brothers, known as the Maccabees, formed an army and were successful in reclaiming the Temple, which had been vandalized. When Judah and his brothers were finished cleaning it up, they wanted to light an oil lamp, but there was only enough oil to last for one day. Miraculously, the lamp burned for eight days. Chanukah lasts eight days to commemorate the burning of the oil.

Collaborator: an individual who supported and assisted the Nazis to impose anti-Semitism. Examples included journalists, lawyers, judges, authors, civil servants, and even everyday citizens who not only refused to come to the aid of Jews, but actively assisted the Nazis in enforcing their rule.

Concentration Camp: set up by the Nazis to imprison those they believed were "undesirable," such as Jews, Roma, homosexuals, political dissidents, and Communists. Hitler established more than one hundred major concentration camps and several thousand smaller camps.

Dachau: the first Nazi concentration camp, located near the German town of Dachau. It served as a camp for political prisoners, those who opposed the policies of the Nazi government, and also served as the blueprint and model for the all the concentration camps that followed.

Death/Extermination Camp: a concentration camp utilized for the sole purpose of murdering camp inmates. Most were located in Poland. Auschwitz-Birkenau, Belzec, Chelmno, Majdanek, Sobibor, and Treblinka were death camps that were instrumental in carrying out the Final Solution and the Nazi plan to murder all European Jews.

Death March: the forced march of prisoners across long distances with no provisions. In 1944, as the Allied forces were advancing toward Nazi concentration camps, guards moved to destroy the evidence of their crimes while inmates (the vast majority being Jewish) were marched toward Germany. Prisoners who had endured the camps were then forced to march for days with no food, through snow and freezing temperatures. Those too weak to continue were shot.

Discrimination: the result of individual and/or group prejudices. Forms of discrimination can range from openly rejecting or taking advantage of another group all the way to genocide, as in the case of European Jews. The reasons for discrimination usually make no sense, but are based on differences in race, religion, or nationality.

Final Solution: the term given to the Nazi plan to murder all European Jews.

Ghetto: a walled-off portion of a city in which Jews were forced to live. Living conditions were terrible, with no sanitation and very little food. As a result, many died of disease or starvation. Ghettos also made it more convenient for the Nazis to deport Jews to labor and death camps. During the Second World War, the Nazis established more than three hundred ghettos in Poland, the Soviet Union, the Baltic States, Czechoslovakia, Romania, and Hungary.

Genocide: the deliberate and systematic extermination of a national, racial, political, or cultural group.

Gestapo: security police used by the Nazis to monitor, protect, and stamp out any opposition to the Third Reich. The Gestapo could arrest anyone whose behavior might be contrary to Hitler's political position. They also were responsible for setting up and administering the concentration camps.

Hitler Youth: known in German as *Hitler-Jugend*, a group organized for German male children between the ages of 14-18. Members were given military training and instructed in anti-Semitism. One of the main goals of the organization was to prepare male youth for eventual service in the German army, to fight for the Nazi cause. The group was founded in 1922 and by 1936 membership was compulsory.

International Holocaust Remembrance Day: the day designated by the United Nations as a day of remembrance for the victims of the Holocaust. Since November 2005, January 27th has been observed as an international day of Holocaust remembrance.

Holocaust Memorial Days: the days of Holocaust remembrance designated by various countries around the world. For example, in Israel, Holocaust Remembrance Day or *Yom HaShoah* occurs on April 27 and is commemorated by a service at Yad Vashem (see below).

Jehovah's Witness: a denomination of Christianity whose members defied the Nazi regime, refusing to give up their religious beliefs, resulting in their deportation to concentration camps.

Joseph Mengele: also known as the "Angel of Death," was a doctor at Auschwitz-Birkenau concentration camp responsible for the selection process that occurred with each new arrival of prisoners to the camp. He decided who was sent directly to the gas chamber and who was sent into back-breaking forced labor. He was also notorious for cruel experiments carried out on camp inmates (mainly Jews). He escaped to Argentina at the end of the war and died in an accidental drowning in Brazil.

Kindertransport: the rescue efforts to save nearly 10,000 young Jewish children by taking them from Nazi Germany, Poland, Czechoslovakia, and Austria to England between 1938 and 1940. After the war, only a small minority was reunited with their parents, most of whom were murdered in Nazis concentration camps.

Kristallnacht: the "Night of Broken Glass" took place in Austria and Germany on November 9–10, 1938, and was orchestrated by Josef Goebbels, the Nazi Chief of Propaganda. Mobs targeted Jewish homes and businesses, looting, stealing, and smashing windows. Synagogues were burned, and Jews were beaten, humiliated in the streets, and murdered; 30,000 more were arrested and deported to concentration camps. Sadly, after this event, many Jews who attempted to flee Europe were unsuccessful because few countries were willing to offer refuge.

Ledor Vador: a Hebrew term that means "from generation to generation" and denotes a central belief in Judaism; to pass on tradition and customs from one generation to the next.

Liberation: the freeing of countries, ghettos, and concentration camps from Nazi occupation. The Allied troops liberated the ghettos and concentration camps in 1944 and1945.

*Magen David/*Star of David: a six-pointed star or emblem originally used as protection against evil spirits; has become a universal symbol for Judaism. The Nazi party used it to identify Jews, who were forced to wear the Star of David on armbands or badges pinned to their clothing.

Majdanek Concentration Camp: a death camp located near the town of Lublin in Poland. More than 79,000 people were murdered here, most of them Jews. (Also see Death/Extermination Camp.) The Nazis did not have time to destroy Majdanek before the Russian Army liberated the camp in 1944. As a result, it is the most well-preserved of the concentration camps.

Masada: a mountaintop fortress located in the Judean Desert; it is an important symbol in Judaism. Built between 37 and 31 BCE by Herod the Great, it served as a fortress for a group of Jews, known as Sicarii, fighting the Romans between 70 CE and 73 CE. After the Great Revolt and the Roman destruction of the Second Temple in 70 CE, the Sicarii fled to Masada to fight the Romans. When it was realized the fortress would fall, the group committed suicide rather than risk capture and slavery. Today, it symbolizes the decision to choose death over slavery and, as such, has great significance for Jewish cultural identity. It has been designated as a World Heritage Site by UNESCO.

Nazi (National Socialist German Workers' Party): political party headed by Adolf Hitler, which was founded in 1920, took power in Germany in 1933, and was defeated by the Allies in 1945. During this period, it was the only German political party.

Neo-Nazis: groups who believe in the policies of the Nazi Party and express admiration for Adolf Hitler and support for racism, anti-Semitism, and Holocaust denial. There are neo-Nazi supporters around the world.

Pawiak Prison: located in Warsaw, Poland and built in 1835. After the Germans invaded Poland in 1939, it served as a Gestapo prison and then became part of the Warsaw Ghetto. The prison became the Nazi base of operations during the Warsaw Ghetto Uprising. (Also see Warsaw Ghetto.)

Perpetrators: those directly responsible (Hitler, military officials, the SS, Gestapo, etc.) for the discrimination, violence, and murder of those targeted by the Nazis.

Pink Triangle: the badge assigned to homosexual men deported to Nazi concentration camps. Under the concentration camp system, every group deemed "undesirable" (i.e. Jews, homosexuals, Roma, Communists, etc.) was given a symbol, or badge, to be worn as part of their camp uniform.

Prejudice: the act of pre-judging a group or individual based on very little or no knowledge; usually based on a stereotype.

Racism: the irrational belief that race accounts for the difference in human behavior, ability, and intelligence.

Resistance: refers to actions taken by groups and/or individuals who stood up to the Nazis. There were many forms of resistance, from partisan fighting groups to the simple act of showing kindness and compassion to an individual targeted by Nazis. Both Jews and non-Jews took part in acts of resistance.

Rescuers: those who risked their own lives to help save the lives of Jews and other groups, either by hiding them or arranging for their escape from Nazi-occupied territory. Rescuing was also an act of resistance.

Righteous among Nations: (or "Righteous Gentiles") were non-Jews who helped save Jewish lives during the Holocaust. They are recognized at the Yad Vashem memorial in Israel. (See Yad Vashem below).

Roma: a group of people originating in northern India who migrated to Europe in the 14th century and led unconventional lives, drifting from area to area. The Roma was one of the groups targeted by the Third Reich and deported to concentration camps. Typically known as gypsies then, today the politically correct term is Roma.

Scapegoating: blaming and holding an individual or group responsible for problems.

Sabbath: (or *Shabbat*) day of rest in Judaism, which is observed from sunset on Friday until Saturday evening. It symbolizes the seventh day in Genesis.

Shoah: Hebrew word meaning "catastrophe," which refers to the Holocaust.

SS *(Schutzstaffel* or **storm troopers)**: Hitler's elite troops whose responsibilities included the persecution of the Jews, the supervision of the concentration camps, and the enforcement of the Final Solution.

Stereotype: a belief about an individual or group that is based on general and often distorted concepts. The use of stereotypes was often the basis of discrimination against Jews during the Holocaust.

Swastika: the emblem for the Nazi party; it was originally an ancient Indian symbol for peace. It was inverted and is now associated with the evils of the Nazi regime.

Synagogue: a place of worship for those of the Jewish faith.

Torah: the first five books of Moses, which contain the laws of Judaism. In the Christian world, the Torah is recognized as the Old Testament.

Twinning Program: a program in which a modern day Jewish child shares her/his Bat/Bar Mitzvah with a child who perished in the Holocaust. This makes the Bat/Bar Mitzvah experience more meaningful and also serves as remembrance of those children who did not survive the Holocaust.

Transport: refers to the transfer, usually by train, of Jews to labor and death camps.

Ujhel: is a town located in Northern Hungary.

Victim: the intended targets of Nazi aggression; those deemed "undesirable," including Jews, Roma, homosexuals, POWs, political opponents, resisters, the mentally handicapped, and the mentally ill.

Warsaw Ghetto: the largest of the ghettos, established in 1940 in the city of Warsaw in Poland. Almost half a million Jews were imprisoned there in the three years of its operation. Most were transported to the Treblinka death camp where they were gassed. In 1943, when the Nazis were planning the final evacuation of the Warsaw ghetto, there was a mass uprising by a group of Jewish resistance fighters. This became known as the Warsaw Ghetto Uprising.

Yad Vashem: the museum established in 1953 in Jerusalem as Israel's official memorial to Jewish victims of the Holocaust.

Zegota Resistance: a group of Christians who were part of the Polish underground resistance, active from 1942 to 1945. Their main objective was to find safe hiding places for Jews escaping from the Nazis. Irena Sendler overlooked the children's section of the organization. She and her group helped save approximately 9,000 Jewish children, 2,500 of which she personally cared for by smuggling them out of the Warsaw Ghetto, placing them with foster families, orphanages, churches, and convents. At the conclusion of the war, Sendler attempted to reunite families, but found that the majority of parents had been murdered. She was nominated for the Noble Peace Prize in 2008, the same year she passed away.

References

i. www.quotationspage.com/quote/2629.html

ii. *A Class Divided.* Dir. Floyd Freidus. Perf. Judy Woodruff. PBS/ FRONTLINE, 1985. Film.

iii. Kuper, Jack. *Child of the Holocaust.* Toronto: Key Porter Books, 2006 (1967). Print.

iv. Swaim, Alice M. *Beneath a Dancing Star.* Poetic Page, 1991. Print.

v. Frank, Anne. *The Diary of a Young Girl Anne Frank.* London: Viking, 2002. Print.

vi. Ibid

vii. Levine, Karen. *Hana's Suitcase.* Toronto: Second Story Press, 2002. Print.

viii. Lucas, Ryan. "Poland honors 'hero' for saving Jewish kids." Thestar.com, 2007. www.thestar.com/News/article/192067

ix. Quoted in "Holocaust heroine's survival tale" by Adam Easton. BBC News (2005-03-03).

x. Ibid

xi. Kacer, Kathy. *Hiding Edith*, Toronto: Second Story Press, 2006. Print.

xii. *The Courageous Heart of Irena Sendler.* Dir. John Kent Harrison, Perf. Anna Paquin, Marcia Gay Hardin, Goran Visnjic. Hallmark Hall of Fame, 2009. Made for TV movie.

xiii. Bülow, Louis. "Irene Sendler An Unsung Heroine". Web. 19 Sept. 2010. www.auschwitz.dk/sendler.htm

xiv. Martin Luther King, Jr., *Speech at St. Louis*, DGC, 1964. CD.

xv. BBC News. 17 May 2011. British Broadcasting Corporation. 27 October 2011. www.bbc.co.uk/news/world-africa-13431486

xvi. United States Holocaust Memorial Museum. Courtesy of Belarusian State Archive of Documentary Film and Photography. Photograph #38065. www.ushmm.org

xvii. United States Holocaust Memorial Museum. "Children during the Holocaust." *Holocaust Encyclopedia*. 2011. www.ushmm.org

xviii. United States Holocaust Memorial Museum. www.ushmm.org The original print was owned by Tadeusz Mazur and Jerzy Tomaszewski and now resides in Historical Archives in Warsaw. The original German inscription on the back of the photograph reads, "Ukraine 1942, Jewish Action [operation], Ivangorod."

xix. Messenger, Charles. *The Chronological Atlas of World War Two*. New York: MacMillan Pub. Co., 1989. Print.

xx. Wiesenthal, Simon. From www.brainyquote.com/quotes/authors/s/simon_wiesenthal.html

xxi. Wiesenthal, Simon. From www.brainyquote.com/quotes/authors/s/simon_wiesenthal.html

xxii. Wiesenthal, Simon. From www.brainyquote.com/quotes/authors/s/simon_wiesenthal.html

xxiii. Goldman Rubin, Susan. *The Anne Frank Case: Simon Wiesenthal's Search for the Truth*. New York: Holiday House, Inc., 2009. Print.

xxiv. Ibid

xxv. United States Holocaust Memorial Museum. National Archives and Records Administration, College Park, Md. Photograph #26542. www.ushmm.org

xxvi.   Hilberg, Raul. *The Destruction of the European Jews*. New York: (1961) New Viewpoints, 1973. Print.

xxvii.   United States Holocaust Memorial Museum. Photograph #N02456. www.ushmm.org

xxviii.   Matas, Carol. *Daniel's Story*, New York: Scholastic Inc., 1993. Print.

xxix.   Kacer, Kathy. *Clara's War*. Toronto: Second Story Press, 2001. Print.

xxx.   Levine, Karen. *Hana's Suitcase*. Toronto: Second Story Press, 2002. Print.

xxxi.   United States Holocaust Memorial Museum. Courtesy of Belarusian State Archive of Documentary Film and Photography. Photograph #66935A. www.ushmm.org

xxxii.   Yolen, Jane. *The Devil's Arithmetic*. New York: Scholastic, 1988. Print.

xxxiii.   Serraillier, Ian. *The Silver Sword*. London: Jonathan Cape, 1956. Print.

xxxiv.   Langford, P. *Writings and Speeches of Edmund Burke*. Oxford: Clarendon Press. 1981. Print.

xxxv.   Ibid

xxxvi.   Ibid

xxxvii.   www.goodreads.com/quotes/show/107570

xxxviii.   Berenbaum, Michael. *The World Must Know*. Ed. Arnold Kramer. Boston: Little, Brown and Company, 1993.

xxxix.   Martin Luther King, Jr., *Speech at St. Louis*, DGC, 1964. CD.

xl.   *The Diary of Anne Frank*. Dir. Robert Dornhelm. Perf. Ben Kingsley, Brenda Blethyn, Hannah Taylor-Gordon. Touchstone Television, 2001. Film.

xli.   United States Holocaust Memorial Museum. Photograph #33201. www.ushmm.org

Members of the Panel

Karen Krasny, Ph.D is Associate Professor of Language and Literacy at York University in Toronto where she teaches a graduate seminar in Adolescent and Children's Literature and English education to teacher candidates in the Intermediate and Senior Division. Prior to her appointment at York, she worked as a K to 12 teacher and curriculum coordinator in Winnipeg schools and served as Manitoba's Early Years Provincial Language Arts Specialist. *Collection Imagination*, her series of 18 French children's books was widely adopted in elementary French classrooms across Canada and the United States. Dr. Krasny's scholarly research focuses on how readers and writers use imagery and effect to construct meaning in text. She currently holds a three-year grant from the *Social Sciences and Humanities Research Council of Canada* to investigate how diasporic narratives inform an independent national identity in post-Soviet Ukraine. Widely published, Dr. Krasny continues to lecture in countries around the world including Canada, the United States, Mexico, Ukraine, Saudi Arabia, and China.

Susan Gordin is a secondary school English and history teacher with the Toronto District School Board. She was part of a team who researched and developed an anti-bullying and anti-racism curriculum for grades nine and ten. As part of that curriculum, she has taught Holocaust studies to Jewish and non-Jewish students for more than 15 years. She also sat on the Educational Advisory Committee for Students and Teachers against Racism (STAR) and participated in a board-wide equity initiative. In addition, Susan is a lead coach and board member of Future Possibilities Canada, a non-profit organization that enables children to build self esteem and life skills while inspiring them to contribute positively to their communities. She has been actively involved in teaching senior creative writing, and has been part of a judging panel for a Toronto-wide short story contest. She is married, lives in Toronto, and has three daughters.

Alan Gotlib is an elementary school teacher. Educated at the University of Toronto, he holds a Bachelor of Science degree, along with a Bachelor of Education degree, and a Masters degree in Education in the area of curriculum, with an emphasis on teaching the gifted. He has been teaching at the elementary level for 30 years. Of those years, 24 of them have been spent at Claude Watson School for the Arts in Toronto, where he has taught academic subjects and drama to students from Grades 4 through 8. He has written original musical plays dealing with issues such as bullying and racism. Along with these plays, he created study guides for use by teachers before and after their students viewed the plays. Alan has given workshops in Canada and the United States for organizations such as the Ontario School Counsellors' Association and the Michigan Education Association to help teachers use the arts to approach the issue of bullying with their students. He has seen the power of the arts in helping students gain a deeper understanding of important issues in their lives. He is the child of Holocaust survivors.

Shawntelle Nesbitt is a former grade six teacher. She currently designs educational programs that address issues of identity, community, human rights, and social justice using the Holocaust as a case study. Her curriculum materials include teacher resources that accompany Second Story Press's best-selling Holocaust Remembrance and First Nations Series for Young Readers, as well as guides designed for their Kids' Power and Women's Hall of Fame Series. She is currently working on a variety of educational projects. Her materials have been integrated into schools in Canada and the United States. She also conducts in-service professional development seminars for educators related to social justice and human rights education. She recently returned from an international seminar on Holocaust education at Yad Vashem in Jerusalem, Israel.

Here is what some educators had to say about this project:

"A huge thank you once again for the wonderful opportunity. You are changing these kids' lives. We truly appreciate this gift."

— *Linda Liem, Bonaventure Meadows Public School, London, Ontario*

"This exercise has been an excellent lesson on reflecting. The students' responses varied from a surface understanding to a much deeper level of connection and empathy. They have learned a lot from…novels, images, and each other. If anything, they have realized the strength of the people during this time period, and the courage they must have had."

— *Bonnie Moffat, Minesing Central School, Minesing, Ontario*

"Thank-you so much for the opportunity to participate in this project. The students were engaged throughout the entire unit on the Holocaust and I am impressed with the writing they produced."

— *Myrle Edmonds, Fallingbrook Public School, Whitby, Ontario*

"Students really enjoyed this and some even found out things about their families that they didn't know."
— *Beverley Mayer, Kedron Public School, Oshawa, Ontario*

"All of our students who wrote really put their hearts into this. I really appreciate this opportunity on their behalf."
— *Lorraine Edwards, Eugene Reimer Middle School, Abbotsford, British Columbia*

"I can't thank you enough for providing our students with this opportunity. I really believe that this was an experience which will remain with them throughout their lives."
— *Donna Lainchbury, Monsignor Morrison Catholic School, St. Thomas, Ontario*

Participating Schools

Assumption School, Aylmer Ontario

B'nai Shalom Day School, Greensboro, North Carolina

Bonaventure Meadow Public School, London, Ontario

Captain Woollahra Public School, New South Wales, Australia

Downtown Jewish Community School, Toronto, Ontario

Durant Road Elementary School, Raleigh, North Carolina

Eagle Ridge Public School, Ajax, Ontario

École secondaire catholique Père-René-de-Galinée, Cambridge, Ontario

Eugene Reimer Middle School, Abbotsford, British Columbia

Fallingbrook Public School, Whitby, Ontario

Fieldstone Day School, Toronto, Ontario

Forest Hill Public School, Midhurst, Ontario

Glenview Senior Public School, Toronto, Ontario

Gordon B. Attersley Public School, Oshawa, Ontario

Grandview Public School, Oshawa, Ontario

Hamburg Middle School, Hamburg, New York

Harmony Heights Public School, Oshawa, Ontario

Istituto Comprensivo Thiesi, Sardinia, Italy

Jack Chambers Public School, London, Ontario

Jewish People's and Peretz Schools (JPPS), Montreal, Quebec

Kedron Public School, Oshawa, Ontario

LaSalle Public School, LaSalle, Ontario

Leo Baeck Day School (North and South Campus), Toronto, Ontario

MacGregor Public School, Waterloo, Ontario

Minesing Central School, Minesing, Ontario

Monsignor Morrison Catholic School, St. Thomas, Ontario

O.M. MacKillop Public School, Richmond Hill, Ontario

Paul Penna Downtown Jewish Day School, Toronto, Ontario

Pope John Paul II Elementary School, Bolton, Ontario

Princess Anne French Immersion Public School, London, Ontario

Regina Mundi Catholic School, Hamilton, Ontario

Riverview Middle School, Riverview, New Brunswick

Robbins Hebrew Academy, Toronto, Ontario

St. Margaret Mary Catholic Elementary School, Hamilton, Ontario

St. Nicholas Catholic School, Waterloo, Ontario

St. Wilfrid Catholic School, Pickering Ontario

The Study School, Toronto, Ontario

Thornhill Public School, Thornhill, Ontario

Wheatley School, St. Catharines, Ontario

Williamsburg Public School, Whitby, Ontario

Yorkhill Elementary School, Thornhill, Ontario

Acknowledgments

This was a new kind of book for me – a departure from my many books of historical fiction and non-fiction. For the first time, I turned to you, my readers, for help in creating a book of stories, reflections, essays, and drawings that would reflect the events of the Holocaust in a meaningful way.

And what a remarkable job you did! I thank each and every one of you who wrote stories and drew pictures – not only those whose creations are in this book, but also everyone who created a submission. You all contributed something important, and I know you learned something in the process. I hope you continue to read stories about the Holocaust and continue to learn about this critically important time in history. And I hope you all continue to write and draw.

I always say that history stays alive when meaningful stories are passed from generation to generation. By contributing to this book, you have embraced the task of keeping this history alive. Well done!

I am truly grateful to the teachers and teacher/librarians who committed to this project and guided students in the creation of their writing. Without you, this book could never have happened. I know how difficult it is to add one more task to your crowded schedules. But you embraced this one whole heartedly.

To Karen Krasny, Susan Gordin, Alan Gotlib, and Shawntelle Nesbitt – how can I ever thank you for the wisdom, care, dedication, and yes, even humor that you brought to this project. You are truly the dream team of committees. Let's do it again sometime.

To Alex Levin – thank you for your wise words and insights. It's been a pleasure meeting and talking to you. Let's continue the friendship and the discussions.

To Danielle Flax – thank you for all your work in pulling the material together, transposing the stories into a complete document, and assisting in the research on quotes and photographs. You were a tremendous help to me and the committee.

To Margie Wolfe – I just keep thanking you, and this time is no exception. Thank you for supporting my work. Thank you for taking on each and every project that I bring to you. Thank you for your friendship and mentorship.

To Sheba Meland – this is the second time we've worked together and it continues to be a pleasure. Thank you for your sensitive touch in the editing of this book.

To the team at Second Story Press – Emma Rogers, Melissa Kaita, Carolyn Jackson – thank you as always for pulling it all together, for your creative touches, and for keeping my books alive in the public's eye.

And to my family – my husband, Ian Epstein, and my children, Gabi and Jake – I love you all and value the balanced perspective that you always bring to my life.